RETRIBUTION

WRAK-AYYA: THE AGE OF SHADOWS
BOOK NINE

LEIGH ROBERTS

DRAGON WINGS PRESS

CONTENTS

Editing by Joy Sephton http://www.justemagine.biz
Cover design by Cherie Fox http://www.cheriefox.com

Sexual activities or events in this book are intended for adults.

ISBN: 978-1-951528-24-9 (ebook)
ISBN: 978-1-951528-08-9 (paperback)

CHAPTER 1

The night fire outside Kayerm was slowly dying. Dorn and Tarnor, leaders of the Sarnonn still living there, sat enjoying the fading embers. A few clouds overhead blocked the stars from the late evening sky. A coyote howled in the far distance, the only other sound now that the cracking of the flames had faded.

A branch snapped. Dorn and Tarnor both jumped to their feet and spun around.

"What are *you* doing here?" Dorn asked as a figure stepped out of the shadows.

"I have come to speak with my mother," said Akar'Tor.

Dorn and Tarnor looked at each other.

"We thought you were dead. Where have you been?" asked Tarnor.

"I will answer your questions after you answer mine. Where is my mother?"

"Your mother is dead. She killed herself. You should not have stayed away so long," snapped Tarnor.

Akar'Tor stumbled backward. "I do not believe you."

"That is up to you, but it is true. Haan came back with her body. We held the final ritual for her. Barely. It was rushed—as if he could not wait to be done with her."

"*Where is my father, then?*"

"He left. With Haaka and your *PetaQ sister*—if that is what you call that thing. They have gone to help the Akassa. Your father is more interested in helping *them* than us. As a result, they are no longer welcome here, nor are you."

Tarnor stepped toward Akar'Tor, who was no match for any Sarnonn.

Akar'Tor put his palms up and backed away carefully. Dorn and Tarnor watched as he slipped back into the shadows.

Dorn looked over at Tarnor, "Why did you let him live? He is of no use to us; he's just a loose end."

"Loose ends sometimes have a way of tying things up later. He may be of use to us, after all. For one thing, he knows the location of Kthama. *Quat.* I may have been too hasty in my rejection of him," he snarled.

"Yes. That was perhaps rash. We do not know where Kthama is. Only Haan, Yar, and a few others do—and they have joined his side. You know as well as I that the whereabouts of Kthama was cloaked to us by the Fathers-Of-Us-All. Haan only found it through his so-called mate, Hakani, who stopped one of their sentries and learned the way back. We have known of it, but never the location."

"Where has that *Soltark*, Akar'Tor, been all this time? I know they searched for him. If he were hurt as bad as was said, someone must have been helping him. The question is who—and is that person still here on our side, or have they gone with Haan?" wondered Tarnor.

"At least you have given him reason to be angry with his father and the others. Perhaps that was wise. If he does come back, let us take a different tack, though. After all, *the enemy of my enemy is my friend*."

Akar'Tor made his way back to the cave where he had kept Tehya captive, the faint crescent moon just enough to light his way. After she escaped, he had left only briefly. His guess was right; they had never returned when they failed to find him there during their first few searches.

Akar'Tor gathered up sticks and branches on the way, and once inside, pulled the stone boulder closed, then packed fir branches in around the cracks to try to keep any sign of the fire from outside, leaving only a tiny crack for ventilation. After the fire was going in its circle of stones, he sat down in front of it. Still lying in the corner was the stone with the dried blood from when Tehya had hit him to make her escape.

My mother is dead? How did she die? I should never have said those things to her; now, I can never make amends. And my father is also gone—with Haaka? Then I am truly alone.

It is my father's fault. He is the one who agreed to go to Kthama. If we had not gone, I would never have realized there was a place where I belonged. He also turned Khon'Tor against me. Everyone is against me, except for Inhrah.

After Tehya had escaped and Akar'Tor's mother found him lying wounded in the cave, Hakani had ordered Inhrah to fetch the Healer, Artadel. But Inhrah had not done so. Instead of going to Kayerm, he had gone into the cave to find Akar'Tor unmoving and curled up in pain.

"Akar, it is me."

"Inhrah. You have to help me!" Akar'Tor moaned, clutching his leg.

"What do you want me to do?" asked Inhrah. "Your mother told me to fetch Artadel to tend to you before we take you back to Kayerm.

"No, Inhrah, I cannot go back. If you are still my friend, you must help me."

"You need something for your wounds."

"Yes, but first you must help me hide. There is a

small supply cave not far down from here. Help me go there and then cover our tracks. Bring Artadel back here with his healing supplies. When he finds me gone, convince him to leave the supplies on the off-chance that I return. Tell him you will regularly come back and check. After a few days, they will stop looking, and you can help me back here."

"But you could die between now and then. It is better that I do as Hakani asked."

"No! My mother has turned on me; you are the only friend I have. It is the only way, trust me. Do not let me down now, I beg you; we have been friends since we were little!" Akar'Tor watched Inhrah's face carefully for his reaction.

"If I do as you say, if you do not get better tending to your wounds, do you promise I can bring Artadel back here to tend to you?"

"I promise," said Akar'Tor.

So Inhrah had done as his friend asked. When he returned with Artadel, and there was no sign of Akar'Tor, Inhrah had asked the Healer how to use the healing supplies and promised to come back to the cave daily to see if Akar'Tor had returned. Always quiet, never causing any trouble, Inhrah had not given Artadel any reason to distrust him. The Healer had Hakani's burial ritual to prepare for, and his loyalty was to Haan rather than Akar'Tor—a reprobate who had kidnapped and endangered a female ripe with offling.

Over time, the Sarnonn did stop looking for

Akar'Tor. Inhrah tended to him and brought him wood, food, and water. He made sure to move stealthily, but luckily the cave was tucked away from the traveled routes.

At first, Akar'Tor could barely walk. In time, though, his wounds healed, and the hair grew back to cover the scars on his legs, for which he was grateful. Gratitude may have been an odd reaction to the situation, but Akar'Tor was also glad that Tehya had only brought the stone down on his leg and not his knee—which could have crippled him for life. She was small, and so was the stone she had hefted, so in the end, he had ended up with a bruise. The overwhelming pain when the rock had hit the open wounds left by the wolf was what had bought her time to get away.

Akar'Tor had plenty of time to think and planning his revenge had become his favorite pastime. He did not know how, but he would make them all pay for betraying him—his father, Haan, the mighty Khon'Tor, and even the High Protector, Acaraho. And somehow—somehow—*Tehya would still be his.*

Everywhere was a flurry of activity. Haan, Artadel, and Haaka were meeting with the Akassa Leaders to learn more about the People's organization and culture. It would require a great deal of change on their part, but Haan was confident that the timing was right. It was obvious to him that the People were far more prepared, structured, productive, and free of incidental toil than Sarnonn culture allowed. In all the People's ways, he saw forethought, planning, balance, and counterbalance. The Sarnonn had already adopted the People's leadership structure with Haan as First Rank and Artadel the Healer as Second. Once Haan and Haaka were paired, Haaka would be Third Rank. From the rest, the Leader had selected a First Guard, and a 'first female' who would function as the head of the females, though it was not an official role. He wished they had a Healer's Helper; he wasn't comfortable with Artadel being the only one with Healer knowledge, though he knew the People's Healers would weigh in if needed.

The Brothers' village was still recovering from Chief Ogima's passing, but looking forward to the bonding of Acise and Oh'Dar. With the help of Acise, Snana, and Noshoba, Oh'Dar had spent the past few days gathering as many beautiful stones from the riverbeds as he could. The spring melt was causing the waters to wash up new ones, so there was a never-ending supply. They sorted them by color, black, white, the autumn colors, and the jewel-like bright ones that mirrored those of some of the birds. He knew Tehya favored the ambers, rusts, and browns; they suited her coloring perfectly. He was not sure of Kurak'Kahn's mate and hoped he would have an opportunity to approach the Overseer before the ceremony. If not, he would have to guess what stones she might like.

He was also working on a different project, a gift for Kalli. He had never made anything like it, and he could see from Snana's reaction as she watched him finish it that it would be a nice surprise.

Time passed, and the village had completed the separate living shelter for Oh'Dar and Acise. She, Honovi, and the other women had done the decorating. The couple would not occupy it until the night of their bonding ceremony; Oh'Dar stood fast on this. He believed in the sanctity of the first mating and was resolute on waiting, despite Acise's coy temptations and flirtatious moves.

Oh'Dar needed to return to Kthama before the ceremony. He still wanted someone to share with him the wisdom of the Ashwea Tare—the secrets handed down by the males about how to please the female and spark her desire so she readily came to her mate.

The saddlebags were full. Oh'Dar made a big deal of thanking Noshoba and Snana. To reward them, he unwrapped a present for each. For Noshoba, there was a carved stallion, darkened in the fire—his own, personal Storm. For Snana, he had picked out her favorite stones, and with her mother's blessing, had made her a demure necklace of her very own. Even though Snana was no longer a child, at seeing her gift she had squealed for joy just as much as Noshoba did. Acise looked at her soon-to-be mate, and her heart swelled with love for him. He had been so thoughtful, and so generous with his time in making these gifts for her siblings.

Oh'Dar hoisted himself up onto Storm. "I will be back as soon as I can; we have so much going on in both places. Are you sure you will not come with me?"

"I want to, but I cannot leave all this preparation for my mother. I did not think it would be this big a ritual, but I guess now that my father is Chief, it is."

Oh'Dar was taken aback. He had not thought about the fact that Acise was now the daughter of the First Chief. *This is not going to help smooth things over with Pajackok,* he thought. *I did not think it through, and I wonder if any of that figured into Pajackok's anger at not winning her?*

Acise waved goodbye and blew him a kiss as he took off for Kthama.

The others were already waiting for him. "Where is Acise?" asked his father, as Oh'Dar rode in on Storm. "You have not run her off already, have you?" he teased.

"She is busy with female things, Father. She is the daughter of a Chief now. I had not really thought about that."

After he had dismounted, Oh'Dar unhooked the heavy saddlebags and let them slide to the floor. "I need to find Kurak'Kahn. I brought beads back for him and want him to pick the colors for his mate's necklace."

Acaraho leaned over and easily picked up the bags.

"First, let me tend to Storm, and I will be right back," said Oh'Dar, and the High Protector nodded that he would wait.

When Oh'Dar returned, Acaraho told him, "The Overseer will be pleased you remembered his request."

Oh'Dar paused a moment, looking off in the distance, hesitating to tell his father what was really on his mind.

"Father, I need help with something."

Acaraho stopped walking and turned to face his Waschini son.

"I am to be paired with Acise soon, at the new moon. And I do not know what to do. I know the mechanics, and I am pretty sure I know how to flirt, as I have seen you and mother do, and sometimes, Khon'Tor and Tehya. From their reactions, the females seem to like to be teased. Playful? I do not know what the right word is, and I would like to learn what else pleases them. The Ashwea Tare—" His voice drifted off.

"Of course; my apologies, Oh'Dar. You are of the

People, and you have every right to the Ashwea Tare. I will make the arrangements."

Oh'Dar nodded gratefully, then asked, "Will I learn—will it work with one of the Brothers' females?"

Acaraho suppressed a smile. He did not want to embarrass his son. "Yes, it will. Despite our differences, females are females and males are pretty much males. After you are through the Ashwea Tare, you will have confidence in how to please her, and not just physically. Because with females, taking the time to create a slow burn results in the hottest flame."

Oh'Dar hung his head, a little embarrassed. "Thank you, Father."

Acaraho put a hand on his son's shoulder and they continued, Acaraho inwardly kicking himself for forgetting this very important rite of passage. Waschini or not, Oh'Dar was one of the People.

They went to the workshop and Oh'Dar showed Acaraho where to set the heavy bags—out of the way of the females who had taken over the room for their designs.

"For now, everyone is busy planning the upcoming celebration. There will be much to tell them, including your pairing and that of Haan and the female, Haaka, whom he has chosen as his new mate. The High Council members will still be here, and they will pronounce Ashwea Awhidi over you and Acise, as well as Haan and Haaka, if they want it.

If they do, they will be the first Sarnonn to take part in a paring ceremony of the People. We are also going to announce that your mother is seeded."

"I think we forget something very important."

Acaraho tilted his head, 'What is that, son?"

"Other than Ithua, Acise, and Honovi, who among the Brothers has seen a Sarnonn in person?"

Acaraho raised his eyebrows. "Good point. Yes. That could be a shock. We must make sure anyone Is'Taqa is bringing will be forewarned. We are living in mystical times, to be sure."

Over the next few days, Oh'Dar found time to speak with Kurak'Kahn and have him pick out the colors for his mate's necklace. He did the same with Khon'-Tor, making sure there were adequate and equal numbers of the best stones in each of the piles from which they would choose. Once again, it touched Oh'Dar's heart to see such an alpha male as Khon'Tor absorbed in picking out just the right colors in just the right combination, in hopes of pleasing his mate.

Lastly, he asked Haan to do the same.

"I am not sure, Oh'Dar. The Sassen do not wear loops of adornment," said Haan, gingerly holding the colorful stones.

"Haaka is a female, Haan. I have it on good

authority that females are very similar all around; they like pretty things. What can it hurt?"

Haan shrugged, not convinced, and went about picking out some larger stones. As a compromise, Oh'Dar offered to make it less ornate than Tehya's. Haan seemed to accept and nodded in agreement; they had a deal, and the young man settled down to start weaving the necklaces. Unbeknown to Acise, he had asked Honovi to pick out some for her as well.

As a show of unity between the Sarnonn and the People, Haan had agreed to take part in the People's pairing ceremony.

It was drawing close. The females were busy preparing various extra foodstuffs that would keep, so they would not be tied to the food area when the festivities began. Extra baskets of water were brought in—anything to cut down on the mechanics required to run in the background once the celebration started.

Dried flowers adorned the front of the Great Chamber. Areas had been cleared for Haan and the few of his people he wanted in attendance. The order of proceedings had been agreed upon. All that needed to happen now was for Acise and Oh'Dar to be bonded at the village. Straight afterward, Acise's parents would return with the new couple to Kthama for the High Council Overseer, Kurak'Kahn, to say the Ashwea Awhidi over them.

The list of attendees was growing. Chief Is'Taqa and Honovi were bringing a select compliment with them. Part of their ceremonial bonding ritual involved chanting and drumming, and they would be introducing this to the Ashwea Awhidi. It was a momentous occasion; since the Age of Darkness, there had been no known contact between the Sarnonn and any community of the Brothers. The celebration would be a historic gesture of unification between them all—the People, the Brothers, and the Sarnonn.

Oh'Dar woke up very early with a start of joy. He rose and wandered down the hallway from his quarters to find his mother and father.

"You look rested, son," said Acaraho. "I am surprised you could sleep the night before you are to be paired."

"I feel more confident now that I completed the Ashwea Tare. It was very helpful, Father. I am still anxious, but now it is more excitement than nervousness."

Adia smiled at her son. She had not been sure if this day would ever come for him, and she and Acaraho were both thrilled that things had worked out for the couple.

"We are ready to leave for the Brothers' Village," she told him.

"Good; they will start as soon as we arrive. Are Khon'Tor and Tehya coming?" he asked tentatively.

"Yes, they are. It will be the largest number of us ever to be there at the same time."

Acaraho had doubled the watchers in the area. Though no Waschini had passed through the Brothers' territory in a long time, he was not taking any chances with some of the People being there in broad daylight. But, as they readied themselves to leave, he had to admit that he was more concerned about the potential Sarnonn threat from those still at Kayerm. Haan had said the location of Kthama was not known to the Sarnonn rebels, but Acaraho did not know if they knew where the Brother's village was. An attack at this time with so much of their leadership assembled together and distracted could be doubly disastrous.

Honovi was assisting Acise as she got ready, brushing her eldest daughter's long black hair and helping her dress. Though she suspected that Acise and Oh'Dar would spend most of their time with the Brothers, helping her prepare to become a life-walker was still bittersweet. Acise raised her arms as her mother slid the beautiful, light buckskin dress down over her head and tugged it into place.

"Are you nervous?"

"Maybe a little," laughed Acise as she smoothed down the dress.

"I am very happy for you, my daughter. You have

chosen well. Oh'Dar will be a great provider, and it is clear you love each other very much."

"I am not in a rush to have offspring, but when we do, I hope they will have his blue eyes!"

Honovi wondered if that might be a possibility since Acise was herself part Waschini. But she secretly hoped it was not. She still had some nagging reservations about having a full Waschini living at the village, but she knew in her heart that Acise would be happy with no other, so she kept her concerns to herself. Now that her daughter had made her choice, Honovi would do nothing to detract from her joy.

The village center was filled, everyone bristling with anticipation not only for the ceremony but for the arrival of the People. Before too long, Oh'Dar showed up on Storm, followed by Khon'Tor, Tehya, Adia, and Acaraho on foot.

Oh'Dar dismounted and was greeted by Honovi. He looked around for Acise, then realized she was probably still preparing in the shelter.

The eyes of all the villagers followed the People as they slowly entered and took their places. None of the Brothers had ever seen so many of the People together at one time—and in the full light of day. Their presence added to the momentous importance of the occasion, and parents whispered to their children to pay attention as this was a day of which future generations would speak in reverent tones.

Once everyone was assembled, the drummers began the beat of the bonding ritual, and soon chanting voices joined in. Acise and Oh'Dar stepped into their appointed places, facing each other and flanked on one side by Chief Is'Taqa, Honovi and the rest of Acise's family. Assembled on the other side were Oh'Dar's people. Though the focus was on the ceremony at hand, many of the Brothers continued to steal furtive glances at them.

When the drums silenced, Chief Is'Taqa raised his staff, and as he spoke, wove it ceremoniously through the air. A flurry of drumbeats punctuated each pause in his proclamation. "Today is a day of great celebration. Today my eldest daughter, Acise, will be bonded with Oh'Dar of the People. I ask the Great Spirit for blessings on them. Let us also recognize the significance of this union as a joining of our people with the People of the High Rocks."

Oh'Dar looked at Acise, no longer the little girl who used to throw acorns at him across the fire. Her gleaming black hair was splayed out over her shoulders like a raven's wing. Her eyes looked up into his, her dark eyelashes fringing her deep brown eyes. Her ceremonial dress was of the lightest hide and adorned with many sparkling beads. In comparison, Oh'Dar was dressed in dark skins, as close to black as he could make them. The contrast between them was striking and memorable.

Chief Is'Taqa joined Acise and Oh'Dar's hands together and raised them. Drumbeats and chanting started up again until, abruptly, silence fell. Again, a short burst of drumming followed each new statement made by the Chief. "May your love last all of your days. May you grow wise together. May you be blessed with many children."

Then Chief Is'Taqa lowered his staff, and the drumming rose in fervor, signaling that Acise and Oh'Dar were now joined together.

Many of the young men and women began circling in dance. Happy conversation started up, rising to be heard above the drums.

Village members came up to congratulate Acise and Oh'Dar, among them Pajackok's father. As Chief Is'Taqa watched them chatting, he scanned the crowd looking for Pajackok himself, but to no avail. Amid the crowd, Ithua looked on with mixed feelings at seeing her brother Is'Taqa stepping into his role as Chief now that her beloved, Chief Ogima, had passed from Etera. She tried discreetly to wipe the tears away—tears of happiness for the young couple mingled with tears of regret that she had cost herself and Chief Ogima their chance at love.

Snana glanced at one of her friends, and the two girls exchanged sheepish grins, both trying to imagine what would take place between the new couple when they were next alone together.

As the congratulations were almost finished, one of the braves slipped away and came back again, doing his best to conceal something squirmy that he discreetly handed to Khon'Tor.

The Leader then turned to Oh'Dar. "Here; this seems as good a time as any to repay Tehya's debt for stealing Kweeuu," and he pushed the gift, a fluffy wolf cub, toward Oh'Dar.

Oh'Dar took the cub and laughed as it struggled to cover him in kisses.

Acise petted the bundle of fur and smiled. "Our first child!" she proclaimed.

"That did not take as much time as I thought it would," laughed Oh'Dar. He lifted the cub to check, "It is female."

"Yes. I thought you might want to start your own pack," said Khon'Tor. "You should let your new mate name this one, though," he added, the joke being that Oh'Dar had unimaginatively named Kweeuu with the word that meant *wolf*.

Everyone laughed as goodwill, and happiness filled the moment for everyone looking on.

Adia stood, her fingers laced in Acaraho's, watching the Waschini offspring she had rescued, oh so long ago, now standing full-grown in a moment she had feared would never come for him.

Acaraho looked down at his mate, "He has found love, just as we have. I know how hard you worked, how much you suffered and endured to get him to this place. I know that today your heart is full."

Adia looked up at her mate and squeezed his hand, nodding slowly.

After a little while, much to Acaraho's relief, she suggested that they return to Kthama. She did not want their presence to distract anyone from the enormity of the event.

She embraced Oh'Dar and hugged Acise. "We will be waiting," she told Oh'Dar before they left. "Enjoy yourselves. We will be waiting and when you arrive, we will start the ceremony at the High Rocks."

Above Kthama, the late morning sun enhanced the natural beauty of the meadow, which had continued its early blossoming. Wildflowers profusely bloomed and their fragrance filled the air, as bees and dragonflies darted about. The fruit trees were in full blossom. Facing each other, Haan and Haaka stood in the center of a circle of Sarnonn. The females were positioned behind Haaka and the males behind Haan.

The Sarnonn began their pairing chant, their voices silencing the wildlife in the area. A doe and her fawn lifted their heads to watch from behind the trees. Ancient words, spoken together in a rhythmic pattern, were almost hypnotic. Haan closed his eyes, letting himself get lost in the meditative droning. When it was finished, he opened his eyes and looked at Haaka.

He gently placed his hand on her head and looked down into her eyes. "I Haan, Leader of the Sassen of Kthama Minor, choose you over all others."

Haaka met his gaze and placed her hand over Haan's heart and repeated, "I Haaka, daughter of the House of Kayerm, choose you over all others."

It was simple and quick. Haan had kept to the standard exchange, not wanting to make a speech that would diminish their new start together by bringing up anything of the past or future challenges. He wanted this moment to have the single focus of their joining; Haaka deserved that.

As had taken place at the Brothers' village with Oh'Dar and Acise's bonding, the others came up to congratulate them and give them their blessings.

After a while, it was time to travel to Kthama. Haan had picked out a handful of his followers to attend the celebration there, among which were Artadel, his Healer and Yar, his messenger. He had made a point of not inviting the twelve Sarnonn whose coats were transformed to silver during the process of opening Kthama Minor for fear of their appearance drawing all the attention away from the ceremony at Kthama.

Haan had a theory of the meaning of the transformation, which he suspected others shared, but for now, he kept it to himself. He was anxious to meet alone with the twelve and felt he was remiss in not yet having made this happen. If they had noticed any other changes in themselves, they had not mentioned them, though he had often seen them talking together. He knew the rest of his group also had questions and hoped it would not be long before the answers became apparent. There were other changes too, changes he had not mentioned to anyone else. A great power had been awakened by the energy released when the Sarnonn opened Kthama Minor and was silently simmering far beneath the cave systems. But all that would have to wait, at least for today.

Khon'Tor and the others entered the Great Chamber to find the air already filled with excitement, everyone milling around chatting. Acaraho had a messenger ready to notify Haan and Haaka once the Brothers arrived. He and Mapiya would meet with them first to explain the order of events before sending for the Sarnonn. The High Protector knew that once the Sarnonn entered, the focus would unavoidably shift to them.

Khon'Tor and Tehya went to greet Kurak'Kahn and the High Council members as they entered the Great Chamber—Lesharo'Mok, Leader of the People of the Deep Valley, Harak'Sar, Leader of People of the Far High Hills, and Kurak'Kahn, the High Council Overseer. Bidzel and Yuma'qia, the record keepers, had reluctantly left their work in the Wall of Records and were also in attendance.

Khon'Tor led them all to their seating. "This is a momentous day. For the first time in thousands of years, the Sarnonn, the Brothers, and our people will be reunited."

"So many changes in a short while," said Kurak'Kahn. The other Leaders nodded agreement.

"And more to come, no doubt," added Lesharo'Mok.

"But today, let us focus on the joy at hand," interjected the diminutive Tehya, all smiles. They nodded in agreement. Khon'Tor's blood rose as he noted the males' eyes sweeping over his mate. She had picked out a particularly festive wrap for the ceremony, a beautiful peach-colored contraption with a fringe and tiny flower-like embellishments—one that did nothing to hide her curves. Knowing they found her attractive made his ardor pulse and thicken. He struggled to control his reaction, not for the first time seriously considering the practicality for males of wearing wraps as the females did.

The Great Chamber had been adorned with richly colored rocks, crystals, and dried flowers temporarily borrowed from many of the living spaces. Nearly all of Kthama was in attendance, parents admonishing their offspring to be quiet and telling them about the importance of what they were about to witness.

After a while, word came that Chief Is'Taqa, Oh'Dar, Acise, Honovi, and the rest of their party had arrived. Acaraho and Mapiya went to meet them as planned and led them to the chamber.

Acaraho then sent the messenger to fetch Haan and his group.

As they waited for the Sarnonn to arrive, Kurak'Kahn took his place at the front platform alongside Khon'Tor. To their left were Oh'Dar and

Acise, looking both excited and anxious. All heads turned when Haan and Haaka entered, accompanied by five other Sarnonn.

The two slowly approached the front and stood to Kurak'Kahn's right while Haan's guests found a place to sit off to the side. The rest of the crowd fell silent at the presence of so many Sarnonn among them. The Brothers could not help but stare at the living proof that the Sarnonn still walked Etera. Both the pairing ceremony and the unprecedented historical significance of this event now shrouded the atmosphere with reverence.

Khon'Tor stepped forward, and all eyes turned to the front. With his Leader's Staff in one hand, he raised the other as a signal that the ceremony had begun.

"Greetings to all and welcome to our visitors. Today is a day to remember. Today, we celebrate the joining of two couples. Oh'Dar, son of the People, with Acise, daughter of the Brothers, and Haan, Leader of the Sarnonn, with Haaka, his First Choice. While that alone is occasion enough to celebrate, let us be mindful of the fact that for the first time in our history, the People, Brothers, Waschini, and Sarnonn stand together in unity. When I became Leader of the High Rocks, I imagined there would be challenges, victories, days I would wish never to end, and days I would wish had never begun. But one thing I did not ever envision was this day—that the

Sarnonn, Brothers, and our People would stand together in unity.

"Change has always been difficult for us. And the last few decades have forced us to the brink of what we thought we could endure. But look where else they have brought us. We stand at the dawn of a new tomorrow— united in ways we could never have imagined. I can say almost with certainty that there will be more revelations and challenges as our story continues, but I am confident we will make it through those days as well. Before we move to the ceremony, please would every new mother stand with her offspring and let us give thanks to the Great Spirit for the blessings of new life."

Others looked around the room as the females with little ones stood and were honored. After a few moments, Khon'Tor nodded that they could retake their seats.

Then Khon'Tor indicated the couples standing with him. "Now let us witness the union of these two pairs who are beginning their journeys together. I will hand over the ceremony to the High Council Overseer, Kurak'Kahn, so we may proceed," and Khon'Tor stepped back.

Kurak'Kahn came forward, and on cue, Acise and Oh'Dar, and Haan with Haaka all stepped around to face him. He turned to Acise and Oh'Dar and took a hand of each. He paused for a moment of reverence, then joined their hands together, and they turned to face each other. After another pause, he raised his free hand and pronounced two words very loudly. *Ashwea Awhidi*!

The People of the High Rocks broke into laughter and smiles intermixed with hoots and whistles. Haan and Haaka looked at each other, knowing they were next. Oh'Dar and Acise stepped to the side, exchanging smiles with their parents and others in the audience.

Kurak'Kahn repeated the ceremony with the Sarnonn couple, and again announced *Ashwea Awhidi*.

Knowing that their Leader and his First Choice were now paired, the Sarnonn contingent joined in with the smiles.

Though that was the whole of it, Oh'Dar signaled to Mapiya, who came forward with two items. She handed one to Oh'Dar and the other to Haan.

Oh'Dar turned to Acise, and tears came to her eyes when she saw what he held. She leaned forward so he could place the beautiful sparking creation around her neck. She looked down and admired it, then leaned up and gave him a sweet, quick kiss.

Haan turned to Haaka and lifted the necklace over her head, letting it drape down to hang in place. She looked down and fingered the large, beautiful center stone. Though not as ornate as Acise's, it was striking in its simplicity. Haaka looked around, blushing as much as a Sarnonn could blush, and gave Haan a brief kiss on his cheek. Both Haan and Haaka were now smiling more broadly, massive canines exposed. It looked terrifying, and all watching had to remind themselves that this was a happy facial expression.

As if on cue, the Brothers' drummers let out a brief round of percussion, which caused more excited laughter, and a cheerful din rolled up from the crowd.

Khon'Tor waited for a few moments and held up his hand. Silence fell, and he motioned to Acaraho and Adia to join him on the platform. Once they were in place, Khon'Tor stepped back, and Acaraho addressed the crowd.

"I look out at a sea of familiar faces, and among those, I also see new faces, unfamiliar, but no less important. And like Khon'Tor, there are faces I never expected to see at Kthama, or anywhere else for that matter. Many of you know that Adia, the Healer, and I have been through many trials. There have also been moments of great joy—as when the restriction against the pairing of Healers was revoked, and we were paired. And now we stand here not only as a paired couple but also as a couple excited to announce that we are awaiting the birth of—" *Acaraho caught himself in time before the words 'our first' slipped out*— "an offspring."

The crowd erupted in joy, those near Nootau turning to congratulate him on the impending birth of a sibling.

Khon'Tor waited for the crowd to quiet down before continuing. "One last announcement, and then I promise I will let you carry on with the celebration. As you know, Kthama Minor has been opened. Were it not for Haan and his followers, the secrets of the past—the very existence of Kthama Minor—would have remained hidden from us forever. Our alliance with Haan's people has already proven to be a blessing. Our futures are joined now in ways I cannot go into at this moment. But to that end, Haan's people will be moving into Kthama Minor. This cooperation between our tribes will no doubt enrich both communities. Now, enjoy yourselves, recognizing that you are living in the days our descendants will look upon as legendary."

As Khon'Tor and the others exited the stage, Chief Is'Taqa nodded and the drummers started up again. He and Honovi scurried over to embrace Oh'Dar and Acise and then turned to congratulate Haan and Haaka. Adia and Acaraho joined the circle as well.

Somewhere in all the excitement, one of the Brothers stepped out and started to twirl and circle, arms stretched out, black hair flying. Then another joined him, and another. Before too long, not having the same reservations as the adults, the offspring joined in, and the room was filled with colors in motion. Haaka and Haan were themselves marking the beat, bobbing up and down but staying in place because of their larger size.

Tehya took Khon'Tor by the hand and dragged him into the middle of the crowd. He stood proudly, and with hooded lids, he possessively smiled down at her as she circled and snaked around him, laughing and enjoying the high spirits, the fringe of her skirt bouncing about. Caught up in the moment, Acaraho swooped Adia up and twirled her around until she was laughing so hard that she begged him to stop. As he set her down, Adia was pleased to see Nimida and Tar together off to the side, smiling in close conversation.

The afternoon was filled with socializing and lightheartedness. The females took turns admiring the necklaces of both Acise and Haaka. Even the High Council Leaders stayed and mingled among the others. Seeing an opening, Oh'Dar went over to Mapiya for a moment and collected something from her. He then approached Kurak'Kahn with the necklace he had made for the Overseer's mate.

Kurak'Kahn opened the little pouch Oh'Dar had especially made for it and held up the piece, admiring how it caught the light. Oh'Dar was touched to see a smile cross the Overseer's face.

"Well done, Oh'Dar. It is beautiful; she will be greatly pleased."

"You are welcome, Overseer."

"What service do I owe you in return?" asked Kurak'Kahn.

"Nothing, Overseer. It was my honor to make it for you."

"It seems the females are quite taken with your work. I see a busy future for you, son."

Oh'Dar was touched by the familiar use of the term *son*. It was not so much an expression of affection, but an acknowledgement from the Overseer that Oh'Dar was one of the People.

Adia came over and also admired the handiwork.

Oh'Dar could see that his mother looked very tired. "Mama, you and Father should go and find some private time. It is almost dark, and I will be leaving soon with Acise. But I will be back before too long, I promise."

Urilla Wuti joined the circle, and it was apparent that she was exhausted too. Looking from one to the other he said, "I think you both need to rest."

Bidzel and Yuma'qia sat together in the hubbub, rapidly discussing how best to do justice to the recording of the day's historic event on the People's less ancient wall of markings.

The record-keepers had made more progress on understanding the array of symbols on the Wall of Records at Kthama Minor. They wanted urgently to speak with the High Council about merging their sense of these with the information that already existed at Kthama. To move forward with any plans to solve their problem—and that of the Sarnonn—they would have to consider both sets of records. And just as they had discovered that Harak'Sar's line from the Far High Hills contained Waschini blood, the Wall had given up another surprise they were anxious to share.

After the event had quieted down, Chief Is'Taqa

and the rest of the Brothers prepared to return to their village. Both Snana and Noshoba were exhausted from the excitement, and their parents were anxious to get them home.

As they headed out, Haan and Haaka were taking their leave of Khon'Tor and Tehya.

Khon'Tor addressed the Sarnonn Leader, "This marks a new beginning for both our people. I believe it was fitting." He paused. "Have you given thought to a new name for Kthama Minor?"

"I have. Kht'shWea."

Khon'Tor thought for a moment, taking in the meaning which combined the phrase for *new home* with that of *new start*. He nodded his approval. "It is well-chosen," he stated.

The Leaders exchanged the Sarnonn gesture of greeting and parting, after which Haan with his new mate and his followers left Kthama for their first collective night at Kht'shWea.

Acaraho, Adia, and Urilla Wuti joined Khon'Tor and Tehya and watched the others leave. Acaraho unconsciously breathed a sigh of relief.

Khon'Tor spoke. "I see now that celebration is more important than I had realized. Let us also remember this day for that lesson."

"I will be retiring," said Urilla Wuti. "But I am honored to have been a part of this, and I feel that my continued presence here, for the time being, is somehow important. I am fortunate that my brother's daughter can manage the role of Healer back at the Far High Hills."

"I am thrilled you are still here, Urilla Wuti," said Tehya, embracing her.

"Adia is also tired; we are turning in." Then Acaraho turned to Adia, "Did I make you ill twirling you around? I am sorry; I was not thinking."

"No, that is not it. It is something else. A shift again."

"Like you had before the Sarnonn opened Kthama Minor?"

"Yes. Though I know now what it is."

Acaraho let out a frustrated sigh. He had surmised that this was what Adia was experiencing. She had explained it before as someone reaching out to her from the Corridor. He knew it was part of her life as a Healer—part of her calling—but he was still not comfortable with these occurrences. In fact, he was starting to hate them.

"Do you need to be alone?"

"I think Urilla Wuti and I need to go to her quarters for a while."

Urilla Wuti nodded, and the three left together, Acaraho escorting the Healers to their destination.

Adia and Urilla Wuti stretched out on adjoining mats in Urilla Wuti's quarters. They quieted themselves, and the uneasiness faded as they surrendered to what they recognized as E'ranale's pull. Within moments, they were in the familiar grove at E'ranale's side.

The sights, sounds, and feelings were augmented as before, and Adia had to pull her focus away to look up at the Mothoc giant already standing before them—as if she had been waiting. Her dark body-covering shimmered as it had the first time, striking Adia again as being alive in its own right. She squelched the almost overpowering desire to reach out and touch E'ranale, having learned during her first visit that this was not allowed. "I am not sure I will ever get over the wonder of this place," she said.

"I will try to be concise, but there is much for you to know," said E'ranale.

"You know of the Mothoc, and the Guardians— the silver-covered ones. You need to understand the critical roles the Mothoc and the Guardians play in the health of Etera."

"You make it sound like all of Etera itself is alive."

E'ranale smiled.

"Etera is alive. *Everything* is alive because every-thing that exists is created from the living force of the One-Who-Is-Three. Even objects like rocks have the life force in them. It is simply moving so slowly compared to your vibration that you do not think of it in that way. All of creation is engaged in the dance of life, whether we are aware of it or not."

She paused for a moment before continuing, "Everything in existence is made up of the creative life-force, though not everything has consciousness or awareness. And this is a point of confusion because when you say something is *alive,* what you mean is that you perceive that it has some level of awareness."

Adia and Urilla Wuti remained silent, hanging on E'ranale's every word and hoping they would remember it all correctly.

"What you call life and death is the life force, the Aezaitera, moving in and out of your realm like the inhalation and exhalation of breath. This movement —the coming and going of life into your realm— happens at different speeds, based on the lifespan of each creature, but it is always in motion. So you may think of the cycle of life and death on Etera as the life force—the breath of the Great Spirit—entering and leaving your realm. I have explained this before.

"The three aspects of the Great Spirit work together in this ongoing creative act. The Great Heart is the creative substance, love, from which everything is formed. The Great Mind is the unfathomable intellect that effortlessly thinks everything into existence in infinite combinations of complexity and order. Through the Great Will, the loving, creative force of the Great Heart and the exquisite design of the Great Mind are continuously called into being.

"But without the ebbing and flowing of this life force, the Aezaitera, Etera would stagnate and die, just as would your physical body if its breathing were to cease. Etera would not die all at once, but over time, system by system—until the Order of Functions could no longer sustain the pattern, and the intricate, overall structure would collapse."

Adia sneaked a glance at Urilla Wuti, who quickly returned it as if to say, by *the Mother, this is almost too much to take in!*

E'ranale smiled kindly, having seen the exchange, and continued, "The Mothoc play an important role in this movement. The Mothoc are deeply connected to the Three-Who-Is-One, far more than the Sarnonn and the People. Each Mothoc represents a powerful vortex of connection, facilitating the movement of life—the flow of the life force—through the realm of Etera.

"However, the Guardians serve a different role. To understand it, I must explain more about the nature of the life force current."

E'ranale again paused a moment before continuing, knowing the information she was giving them was considerably outside of their present understanding.

"The current of the life force, the Aezaitera, is only positive. There is only one creative power. And it encompasses both the active male and the receptive female traits. And as a result, it has active creative power but is also receptive, which means it is also subject to impressions in your realm. Those impressions can distort or twist the original positive life force."

"Your High Council was right in part; the threat

to Etera does come from the actions, driven by their distorted beliefs, of those you call the Waschini or the White Wasters. There is a threat, and it is far greater than only to the People or the Brothers. The Whites are innovative, but they are headstrong. There is a dangerous distortion brewing among them; they are coming to believe that they are more important than the other offspring of Etera, and this leads to arrogance. Because they value thinking power above everything else, they see themselves as superior and more important than all other creatures. They take what they want and do not work in concert with others or the Great Spirit. They have little humility. In their ignorance and fear, they grab and hoard. And by these thoughts and actions, they cause division, and division creates more division. Greed and exploitation—the belief that there is not enough, which makes them take more than their share—is critically dangerous. Unless they turn and take their place in unity with all creation and the Great Spirit, and stop creating more and more negativity, or distortion, Etera will sicken and die. As their negative influence grows, the risk is that there will not be enough of the Mothoc blood left, pulling in the positive creative force, to offset the spread of their negativity."

Adia and Urilla Wuti stood there before E'ranale, overwhelmed by the enormity of what they were hearing.

"Our time is almost up. But I have a bit more that

I must share with you now. You have heard Haan, the Sarnonn Leader, speak of the Guardians. You have seen the discarded husk of my mate, Moc'Tor, in the tomb within Kthama Minor, now to be called Kht'sh-Wea. The Guardians play a greater role in preserving Etera. The Mothoc can pull in the creative loving-force more strongly than it normally flows, but a Guardian cleanses the distorted Aezaitera circulating in Etera's realm and returns it to its original, positive flow.

"A Guardian is practically immortal, as the cleansing of distortion in the Aezaitera re-enlivens him or her with the positive creative force. But, as the Mothoc blood has left Etera, so the risk to her long-term survival has increased proportionally."

"Go back to your High Council and deliver this information. They must understand the importance of re-establishing the Guardians. Guardians are only born through the 'Tor line, those originally from Kthama and Kayerm, descended from the offling of Moc'Tor and Straf'Tor. Yes, you are thinking of the silver-bodied Sarnonn created when the Sarnonn opened the vortex bringing in the powerful life force to open Kthama Minor. That this would happen was unknown to the Sarnonn. They did not know that a Guardian could be created this way; we allowed it when we closed Kthama Minor and set in motion everything that has brought both tribes to this re-unification. But these new Guardians are not as powerful as a pure Mothoc Guardian. At present, they have no idea of their sacred duty, only that they have been changed. But even though they do not speak of it outside their circle, they are aware that some great power is pulsing, spreading through their internal systems.

"The Guardians created through the opening of Kht'shWea were selected from mated pairs in hopes of producing Guardian offspring. But they were also created for other purposes. One is for the protection of Kthama and Kthama Minor and the powerful vortex that has always existed beneath them, but which has been relatively dormant since the end of the age. When the Seventh arrives to lead the six new male Sassen Guardians, their work of bringing your realm into the Wrak-Ashwea will begin in earnest."

Adia covered her mouth with her hands, a thousand questions poised on her lips. *Wrak-Ashwea? The Age of Light? And why only the males? What of the female Guardians?*

"But, again, they and their offspring must be trained in how to use their abilities for the specific protection of Kthama and Kthama Minor. Perhaps you understand now why there had to be such a division between the Akassa and Sarnonn. The Sarnonn bloodline had to be kept as pure as possible so they would be able to enter the state of Ror'Eckrah. The Ror'Eckrah allowed them to release the amount of creative power needed to open Kthama Minor, and at the same time, from the vortex below, draw the vast amount of Aezaiteric energy necessary to create the new Guardians. Even though somewhat diluted with the Brothers' blood, the Sarnonn are the closest to the original Mothoc. They had to be kept from your people for your protection. Fear, authority, and threats were what they understood, and so they were given the Rah-hora. And the People had to be kept separate from them for fear of diluting the Sarnonn blood further, to keep as much Mothoc blood in the Sarnonn for this moment. For without both sides surviving, later to work together in unity, there would be no hope for the Akassa, the Sarnonn, or Etera."

E'ranale paused.

"Enough of the Sarnonn had finally evolved in their thinking to where you could work together toward creating the future of your own making. It was no longer necessary for you to be kept separate; it was crucial you came together at this appointed time, because, to save Etera, both your tribes must work together from now on. When the seal on the stone blocking Kthama Minor was broken, Wrak-Ayya, the Age of Shadows began, and the Rah-hora was dissolved.

"One last thing. The release of the flood of Aezai-teric energy into your realm caused several changes. Some you have noticed—the influx of life in the meadow used by the Sarnonn and along the path they walked to Kthama Minor, the creation of the Sarnonn Guardians, and the transformation of the granite obelisks into crystal form. Another is the re-awakening of the massive creative vortex that exists under both Kthama and Kthama Minor. There are other powerful vortexes around Etera, but none quite as strong as that one. That vortex contains enormous creative power—it is through this that the Sarnonn harnessed the energy to open Kthama Minor. It must be protected. Some of you are already aware of the increase in the force of this swirling, energetic mass, though you do not know what it is or what it portends. Despite the pull of my calling you here, it is also this force that has caused your unease, Healers. And the increase in your sensitivities and gifts has heightened that feeling."

"That is all I will tell you for now; it will make even more sense to you once certain approaching events are passed. Now, return to your own realm until it is time for us to meet again."

Within moments, Urilla Wuti and Adia were back in their physical bodies in Etera. Exhausted, their minds swirling with what they had just been told, they carefully compared notes to make sure they remembered every bit of what E'ranale had said.

"We need to rest," said Urilla Wuti eventually. "We are in no condition to speak with the High Council as yet."

"Yes, but I cannot get a couple of things off my mind. One is that it sounds as if the Mothoc still live. And what is the Order of Functions? And *who* exactly is supposed to train the new Guardians in their duty to protect Kthama and Kht'shWea?"

'Those, young Healer, are excellent questions.

But the answer is beyond us at the moment, and I am too tired to wrestle with it now."

Adia nodded, and getting comfortable despite their excitement and awe at what they had just experienced, they swiftly drifted off to sleep.

CHAPTER 2

Haan and Haaka walked together down the path to their new home. Kht'shWea had been abuzz with activity off and on. Before they could move in, the Sarnonn had needed to understand the layout and allocate the living spaces, making improvements where they could. They also had sleeping mats, baskets, and food stores to take care of. Though not all the preparations had been finished, it was ready enough, and the community had agreed their first night in their new home would be the night of Haan and Haaka's pairing. Many of his people were waiting outside to greet them, and as they entered, others came up to them and congratulated them further. One of the females passed Kalli into Haaka's arms, and the little offling reached for her new mother.

"I tried to tire her out," said Sastak. Haaka smiled her thanks and tucked Kalli up under her chin.

When the greetings had died down, Haaka gave Kalli back to Sastak so she and Haan could have the evening to themselves. Then they headed for their new quarters. Taking a cue from the People, the Sarnonn females had decorated it with flowers and pretty stones.

Being the Leader's Quarters, it was a spacious area. Arranged much like the quarters at Kthama, a lot of work had gone into creating the ventilation shafts that brought in fresh air and light.

Haaka looked around and spotted the nest created for Kalli. It was in a protected nook and beautifully done. Hanging over it, high enough out of reach, was some type of decorative arrangement with what looked like colorful butterflies and drag-onflies suspended from thin threads.

Haaka looked closer. "This is beautiful. Did you make this?" she asked, immediately realizing he could not have; the workmanship was too fine.

"Oh'Dar of the Akassa made it as a gift for Kalli."

She gently fingered the brightly colored insects, which were made from stylized, dyed, and adorned pieces of hide. They bobbed up and around when she touched them. "That was very kind of Oh'Dar—and he has attached little glimmering stones for their eyes," she exclaimed. "They are remarkable, are they not," she said more as a statement than a question.

While she was still looking at the dancing arrangement, she could feel Haan approaching her slowly from behind. She froze. He placed his hands on her shoulders and peered down at the decoration.

They stood a moment. Haaka's heart was pounding so hard she feared Haan would hear it.

Haan slowly turned Haaka to face him. She looked into his eyes and swallowed hard. He leaned over and kissed her. She snaked her arms up around his neck, surrendering to the pleasure that swept up through her center. He kissed her harder, his desire for her now unmistakable and taking the forefront of his consciousness.

He took her hand and led her over to the sleeping mat. It was a huge construct, and Haaka found herself thinking how long it must have taken to assemble. Then she realized that, out of fear, she was distracting herself from the moment at hand. *I hope he is not disappointed in me,* she thought. *I have never been mated; I have no experience in this.*

"Haan. I have never— This will be— I mean— You know, this—"

Haan blinked. It should have occurred to him that she was a maiden. It had been a long time for him, but now realizing this, he pushed down his ardor and slowed down his approach.

He sat down and guided her to sit next to him. Then he lay back, and she followed. Now stretched out together side-by-side, he stroked the back of her head and wrapped his arms around her. *It has already been some time. What is a little longer,* he thought to himself.

"You are tired, Haaka. It has been a long and exciting day. Just sleep."

"Are you sure?" she asked. "I know you have been without mating for a long time."

"The pleasure is not for me alone. You must enjoy it too. It can wait. And so can we," declared Haan.

Within moments, relieved and exhausted, Haaka was asleep. Haan lay awake for a while, replaying the day's events. It then hit him that it was nearly a year since Kalli's birth. *Four months since Hakani— How much everything has changed*, he thought. A tinge of guilt washed over him for pairing with Haaka so soon after Hakani's death. However, he had sensed only acceptance from his group, and for that he was grateful.

As he began to relax, no longer distracted by outside events, he became aware of the churning magnetic vortex far beneath the caves of Kht'shWea.

Adia and Urilla Wuti slept through the entire night, but Adia awoke to find her fellow Healer already up and about.

She propped herself up on one elbow and watched. Gaging by the shaft of light coming through the ventilation shaft, it was still early. "Good Morning. I am anxious to talk about what E'ranale told us."

"Yes, we must speak with Khon'Tor's Circle of Counsel and the High Council members. But I feel we should tell Khon'Tor and the others first."

Adia nodded and also rose to meet the day. She seldom slept away from Acaraho and was anxious to go and find him.

"I must get something to eat; come and join me," she said.

Shortly after, the two Healers made their way to the Great Chamber.

Acaraho, Khon'Tor, and Awan were already seated together. Acaraho smiled, relieved at seeing Adia coming his way, even though he had checked in on them in the middle of the night. He rose to greet her and make room next to him as he anxiously assessed what he could of her condition. Adia noticed it, and with a smile, she nodded her reassurance to him as Urilla Wuti sat next to Awan.

"What a celebration," said the older Healer as she set her food down in front of her before sitting. "The drumming and the dancing! I think the Brothers can teach us a thing or two about how to liven up events."

"Where is Tehya?" Adia asked in between mouthfuls.

"She did not sleep well; she is still in our quarters," said Khon'Tor.

"Nightmares, still?"

Khon'Tor nodded. "She is losing weight."

"With your permission, I will go and see her after we finish here," offered Adia.

Khon'Tor nodded but did not answer. *She will not be able to help Tehya. I am the only one who can help her. I am the cause of her nightmares, and only I can provide the solution. And as long as there is a chance Akar is alive, she will continue to suffer. I vowed to protect her, yet how can I when it is my very presence which is keeping her fear alive? Instead of her protector, in the dark she believes her captor, Akar'Tor, is lying next to her.*

Urilla Wuti finished eating. "Adia and I have information to share with you and whomever else you want us to. It has to do with the Wrak-Wavara."

Khon'Tor's head snapped up. He did not question her source; he had accepted that the Healers had abilities he would never understand.

"Send for me after Adia has seen to Tehya. Acaraho, then assemble my Circle of Counsel. We will meet in the usual place."

Acaraho mentally ran through the list of members. Tehya, Adia, Nadiwani, First Guard Awan, Mapiya, who represented the females, and Oh'Dar. "Oh'Dar is still at the village, but he has not been made privy to what the High Council told us about our bloodline problems."

"No doubt whatever the Healer's tell us will be shared with the High Council. If he is back in time, he can hear it when they do—and if there is time beforehand, share what you know with him. I do not wish to wait." Khon'Tor directed.

Before long, the Circle of Counsel was assembled in the usual meeting room.

Adia took the floor. "The information we have been given is critical to understanding the path, or paths, before us. There are certain abilities that some Healers have. Urilla Wuti has these abilities and, through the years, has been teaching me and others to develop them. It is through these special talents that we bring the information we are about to share."

"Who or what is the source of this information?" asked Khon'Tor, though he had sworn he would not.

"Please do not ask us how we received it, as that has no bearing on its validity. You must accept that it is trustworthy and shared entirely for our benefit.

Everyone was listening with rapt attention.

"All of you have seen the bodies in the burial chamber at Kthama Minor. The one named Moc'Tor has a silver body covering. His brother, Straf'Tor, did not. You will remember Haan said that the silver-coated Mothoc are called Guardians, but there is more to the difference than appearance."

Adia paused; there was so much to share that she wasn't sure where to start. She took a deep breath, not wanting to get ahead of herself and create confusion.

"The role of the Mothoc is to augment the flow of creative life force in and out of Etera. Think of it as breathing. The cycle of life and death, taking place at varying rates in every moment, is the life-breath of Etera. The Mothoc act as a center of increased flow for this creative force, which is called the Aezaitera. They are far better connected to the Great Spirit than we are. Far more even than the Sarnonn. The Guardians, however—the silver-coated ones—somehow do not simply help this flow of the creative life force, but they cleanse the Aezaitera of the negativity it picks up within this realm.

"Because the creative force is alive, it can be affected once it enters our level of existence. With their belief that there is never enough, which causes them to take more than they need, the Waschini create division and harm. There are not enough left of the Mothoc or Guardians to counteract this build-up of negativity that then contaminates the Aezaitera flow."

"Contaminates the flow?" asked Nadiwani.

"Yes. And as their numbers grow, the impact will worsen. The Guardians not only augment the flow, but they somehow purify it. As the number of Waschini increases and they spread their perception of scarcity and the influence of their greed, it becomes harder to cleanse the Aezaitera of the nega-tive impact. If their progression is not stopped, in time the Waschini's belief in lack will become a self-fulfilling prophecy and will create true scarcity and dangerous strife—perhaps even wars."

"So there are still Mothoc on Etera. And Guardians," said Khon'Tor.

Everyone remained silent.

"It would seem so," said Acaraho, eyeing his mate carefully for signs of the toll this might be taking on her.

"There is more," said Urilla Wuti. "The Guardians are only born through the 'Tor line. This means only through the descendants of Moc'Tor and Straf'Tor."

Tehya closed her eyes and Urilla Wuti experienced sudden understanding. *She is concerned that with her Waschini blood, whatever slim hope there was that she would ever bear a 'Tor Guardian is gone. She feels she is failing her Leader and mate, and now her people.*

"You are speaking of those here at Kthama and Kayerm, and now Kht'shWea, or Kthama Minor?" clarified Khon'Tor.

Acaraho got up and started pacing. "What of the silver-haired Sarnonn from the meadow? Are they Guardians now? They must have been transformed somehow when the Sarnonn opened Kthama Minor. And also, the twelve granite stones they drove into the ground have become huge crystals. It must have been from the same event."

"Yes," said Adia. "They are indeed Guardians. But they were created for specific reasons—one of which is to protect Kthama and Kht'shWea. We would not have realized this, not knowing Haan's people, but they are six mated pairs."

"So eventually, there will be Guardian offspring?"

"That is the hope," said Adia.

"Does Haan know all this?" interrupted Khon'Tor.

"We were told that the Sarnonn did not know the opening of Kthama Minor would create the new Sarnonn Guardians. Since they did not know that part, I doubt they know any more than we do about the role of the newly created Guardians. However, we were told that when a seventh Guardian joins them, their proper work will begin. We were also told that these new Guardians are not as powerful as the pure Mothoc Guardians."

Acaraho returned to his seat, and they sat for a while, reflecting on what they had just heard.

"Is there more?" asked Khon'Tor.

"They have to be trained. The newly created Guardians have to be trained," said Urilla Wuti.

Khon'Tor frowned, confused. "Trained? Trained in what? And by whom?"

"Trained in how to use their powers—their abilities—for the protection of Kthama and Kthama Minor. And we do not know who will do it," Urilla Wuti answered.

Acaraho stood again. He was agitated, deeply concerned about the effect of this on the health of

Adia and their offspring. "This information implies that the Mothoc Guardians still live," he stated.

Silence.

"You look tired. Is there anything more?" asked Acaraho, his eyes tracing the outline of Adia's face.

Adia told them a little more of what E'ranale said. That the purpose of the Rah-hora had been to keep the People and the Sarnonn apart until they evolved enough to work together. That when the seal on the stone blocking Kthama Minor was broken, the Rah-hora had been dissolved, ushering in Wrak-Ayya, the Age of Shadows.

"We need to share this with the High Council," said Khon'Tor. "And Haan must be there. We should invite Haaka too, as they are paired, and she is now Third Rank. If Oh'Dar is back, have him also attend. It is becoming too difficult to remember who has heard what, and this is no longer the time for secrets. If the Rah-hora has been dissolved, then there is no harm in these revelations being put out on the table for everyone's edification. Commander, call them together as soon as possible."

The group dispersed quickly. Acaraho insisted that Adia come back to their quarters to lie down for a while and suggested Urilla Wuti should also get some rest.

Meanwhile, Bidzel and Yuma'qia continued working on the Wall of Records, which area was avoided by the Sarnonn to leave them undisturbed. They had been given quarters within Kht'shWea but kept to themselves most of the time.

The two record-keepers had made more discoveries and were bursting to share what they had found.

"I do wonder how they are going to take this new information," said Bidzel absentmindedly as he let his eyes wander over the gigantic wall in front of them. They had taken a break and were sitting on the floor, which was soft from the accumulation of the sand of the ages.

"I wonder myself. We are involved in the discovery, but they have to deal with the repercussions; I would rather have our job," said Yuma'qia.

"So little of what we believed has proven true," sighed Bidzel. "It seems everything we uncover shakes a little more of our foundation."

"Better to let that which is built on shifting ground topple, and rebuild on a solid foundation of truth, however difficult."

The High Council assembled with Haan and Haaka also present. Oh'Dar had not yet returned from the Brothers' village, and Adia would tell him later, though what they were learning was increasingly becoming more complex.

The Overseer opened the meeting and then turned it over to Adia and Urilla Wuti. The two Healers repeated what they had shared earlier with Khon'Tor's Circle of Counsel.

When they had finished, they sat down, and the Overseer spoke to those assembled, "I know you have questions. Please take a moment to formulate them clearly before we continue. To preserve order, please stand if you wish to be heard." He turned to Haan and Haaka, who were sitting on the floor next to one of the walls. As he eyed them, he told them, "Please, just wave a hand; there is no need to rise."

After a few moments, despite the Overseer's suggestion, Haan stood.

"The Fathers-of-Us-All have given us a great gift. To have Guardians walk among us once again is a blessing without equal. I suspected as much—that twelve of my people have somehow been transformed into these sacred pillars of service."

"Adia, you were told that these Guardians must be taught how to use their powers. How is that possible? Who will teach them?" the Overseer asked.

"I was not told that. I do not know," said Adia, standing again.

"The logical conclusion is that it is only possible if there are still other Guardians around," snapped Kurak'Kahn.

Adia frowned at the edge in his voice. She had noticed a while ago that the Overseer's patience was growing thin. Perhaps the upheaval of so much they had believed to be true was becoming too much for him.

"Again, Overseer. I do not know for sure. We are only told so much at a time."

"Told by whom, Healer? It is time you tell us the rest of this."

Urilla Wuti stood up and took her place next to Adia.

"The source does not matter, Overseer," she said. "As Adia pointed out, it would anyway do no good to tell you as it could not be proven. You must trust, as we do, that the information is given for our welfare and is true."

"You ask much, Healer," said the Overseer and sat down.

Haan let out a deep breath and said, "I can see the strain is great for you. It was difficult to find that we, your brothers exist. Then to include us now as part of Kthama, to open your community in accepting us. As you know, change has always been difficult for us, the Akassa and the Sassen. But what the Healer says is true; you must accept the information they are giving you. It has brought us this far, and we must trust it will show us the rest of the way. As for the possibility of a teacher for the Guardians, the ancient Mothoc Guardians were practically immortal. The positive flow of the Aezaitera moving through them purifies and extends their life force."

"You are saying the Mothoc are still alive. Or just that the Guardian Mothoc are still alive?"

"You have asked me that before, Overseer," Haan answered. "I do not know. I am only saying it is possible. They have the ability to block our awareness of them."

"As interesting as this is, and with all due respect to the Healers," sneered Kurak'Kahn, "I am starting to think this is all a product of your collective imaginations. Obviously, the Sarnonn exist. And something apparently happened to some of your people, Haan. But the rest of this is too much to accept with nothing to back up your stories."

Adia and Acaraho exchanged looks. Khon'Tor noticed the exchange and read their minds.

"Overseer," he said, "perhaps we should adjourn from here. There is something that you need to see. I regret that there has not been time until now, but I believe this will be of benefit to you and the others as well."

Kurak'Kahn exhaled in exasperation. "Very well."

First Guard Awan opened the meeting room door and stepped aside. As Khon'Tor passed by, he said to Acaraho, "I agree, it is time for them to see the inner Chamber."

Acaraho nodded, and when the others had exited, followed the procession.

He caught up to his mate, "Are you sure you are up to this walk? Do you need me to carry you?"

"I am fine, please."

When the group arrived at Kht'shWea, Khon'Tor halted everyone, and as it was now Haan's domain, let him take the lead.

The entrance to Kht'shWea was no longer empty. Several couples stood talking, and a group of females over to the side were working on creating sleeping mats. They all looked up as the People entered, and several nodded in acknowledgment. The High Council members looked around nervously, not having been in the presence of so many Sarnonn collectively.

Haan led them down the tunnel to the chamber. Their pace slowed as they approached as a feeling of reverence passed over everyone. The Overseer felt it himself, despite not knowing what he was about to witness.

With ease but very carefully, Haan moved the stone at the entrance to the chamber. He entered and stepped aside as they all filed in.

As before, it was dark inside. Their low-light vision engaged at nearly the same time, and there was a gasp, then utter silence as the High Council members stood before the three preserved giants.

Haan approached the figure of Moc'Tor and bowed. Then he turned back to explain to the newcomers what they were seeing.

"This is Moc'Tor. He is the Father-Of-Us-All and was a Guardian. To his left is his mate,

E'ranale. And there is Straf'Tor, brother to Moc'Tor."

The silence in the chamber was deafening. Those outside of Khon'Tor's Circle of Counsel dared not move for fear of breaking the sanctity of where they were. As the others had been when they first stood there, they were overcome by the size of the preserved Mothoc giants seated before them. Their eyes widened as their gazes darted over the figures, taking in as much detail as possible from where they stood.

Finally, the Overseer took a step toward the body of Moc'Tor. He looked it over head to toe, then Kurak-Kahn reached out as if to touch the figure. Haan straightened and bristled, at which the Overseer withdrew his hand. He glanced up and saw the markings carved in the rock wall but said nothing. The others followed his gaze to find the etchings, also remaining silent.

Some time passed before Kurak'Kahn turned to leave. The others followed him, and Haan pushed the boulder back.

The Overseer turned to the High Council members. "Please hold your questions until we return to the meeting room. Come."

As they turned and started back up the tunnel, Bidzel and Yuma'qia emerged from the Wall of Records and stopped them.

"Before you leave, please, we have interesting information to share," said Bidzel excitedly.

"I am tired, but we are here, so show us what you will," said Kurak'Kahn.

The two researchers led the group to the Wall of Records. Much had changed since the last time the High Council was there. A large scaffolding consisting of differently-sized tree trunks had been assembled for them to examine the higher markings. Intercepting the curious glances, Yuma'qia explained, "Haan's people put that together for us. It is a great help and very sturdy—far more secure than we could have constructed, which is important. It would be catastrophic if any of the records were damaged in a fall or collapse."

Yuma'qia stepped into the room, scanned the wall, and having found what he wanted, pointed to a particular set of symbols. "I do not expect you to remember, but this is the line of Moc'Tor's descendants. From this, we can see how many offspring he had, and there are markings we believe indicate which were Guardians and which not. This one here, the youngest daughter, Pan, was a Guardian. But I do not see any others—if we correctly understand this as the mark of a Guardian. At least not full Mothoc Guardians. There are others as the lines mix with the Brothers, but their mark is different, and their numbers dwindle the more the original bloodline is diluted."

Haan agreed, "Yes, that is the Guardian mark. Pan, Moc'Tor's daughter by E'ranale, was the last of the Mothoc Guardians."

"Yuma'qia just said there are other Guardians," the Overseer disagreed.

"There are other striations of Guardian blood, but none is pure Mothoc," explained Bidzel.

The Overseer snorted. "An answer to everything."

"We have extensively studied the lines of both Moc'Tor and Straf'Tor. Because what we have discovered is important, we have gone over and over our findings to be sure there is no mistake."

Seeing that he still had their attention, Bidzel continued, "Perhaps it is because the female Mothoc carried the seed of the Brothers, but after the interbreeding started, the leadership was traced—passed—through the female's line. Not that of the males."

Kurak'Kahn scowled. "Are you saying that the Leaders were *female*?"

"It appears possible, at least in some capacity for some time. It does make sense because that was the only sure way to trace the line since the male seed was coming from the Brothers."

Seeing the disbelief on the Overseer's face, Yuma'qia spoke up in support of Bidzel. "It is true. After their blood was mixed with the Brothers, the records show that the Leaders' lineage was charted through the females. At some point, it reverted to the male line, but we do not know when, because, if records were kept after Kthama Minor was sealed, we do not have access to them."

It was as if everything the Overseer stood on was being pulled out from under him. It was too much—

too much for him to accept in too short a period. Isolated by his station, far from his mate, he had no one to help him bear his burdens. He had barely enough time to process one new piece of information before another one came.

"So, first you tell me that Haan's ancestor and Khon'Tor's were brothers and they are therefore relatives. Then there are these all-powerful Mothoc who planned all of this. You show me a chamber of dried up bodies, supposedly those whose lineage is shown on the wall. And the leadership was passed through the females? This is too much; you have to be mistaken. Not *everything* we have believed can be wrong."

"I know it is difficult, Overseer." Seeing his obvious distress, Adia tried to find words to comfort him.

"It is only difficult if it is true, Healer. I do not accept that everything here is true. I am not doubting that you believe what you are telling us, or that you, Bidzel, and you, Yuma'qia, also believe you are correctly figuring out the markings. But if it is all true, then tell me this. If the Guardians can essentially live forever, *then why is there a dead body of one propped up in that dusty old chamber we just left*? It certainly does not look like there was a struggle. They all just willingly walked in there, sat down, and died?"

For a moment, Bidzel and Yuma'qia looked confused at Kurak'Kahn's mention of the chamber, and then they exchanged wide-eyed glances. From the look on their faces, they had a thousand questions about it but knew better than to raise them now.

The group stared silently at Kurak'Kahn.

Finally, Adia said quietly, "I do not know, Overseer."

"Finally. *You do not know*. Exactly." He started to walk away, then turned sharply and pointed back at them. "And until someone can explain *that* to my satisfaction, I am taking everything you tell us with great reservation."

"It is a fair question," Khon'Tor said to the Healers.

"Just because we do not know the answer to a question, does not mean there is no answer," said Urilla Wuti.

Kurak'Kahn took a few steps back and lowered his face close to hers.

"Well that is convenient, is it not, *Healer*? The perfect statement to dismiss the truth that none of us knows anymore what is real and what is not," he sneered.

Acaraho stepped toward them, "Overseer."

Kurak'Kahn waved him off, "Stand down, Commander. I am done here," he snapped as he looked Urilla Wuti up and down.

Khon'Tor and the others watched as he stormed off.

After a moment, Bidzel spoke up.

"There is more, Adik'Tar 'Tor. If you wish to know," he offered sheepishly. "Or, if you prefer, we can wait for another time."

"No," sighed Khon'Tor. "Proceed."

"Very well. Many of the Mothoc Healers were male. But there were females too. All were allowed to mate and have offspring. There is evidence of this right up to where the records end—again, when Kthama Minor was sealed."

"It seems many of the Mothoc customs changed after Kthama Minor was sealed. It was as if the heritage of an entire culture was purposefully severed," Bidzel added.

"Or divided," said Haan.

"We leave you to the futures of your making," whispered Adia.

Bidzel could contain himself no longer, "You mentioned a chamber?" he blurted out.

Khon'Tor answered absentmindedly, "Yes. Yes, there is a chamber. We have been remiss in not showing it to you. I promise we will. But now is not the time."

Bidzel pursed his lips and kept his silence. Yuma'qia shifted back and forth on his feet, throwing fervid glances at his fellow researcher.

The others again fell silent, and after a few moments, they quietly took leave of Haan to return to Kthama and their various quarters. There was much to think about and much to accept.

CHAPTER 3

Acise and Oh'Dar woke in their new shelter. Acise was curled up against Oh'Dar, and he stretched before wrapping an arm around her waist.

She opened her eyes and smiled. "I slept like a rock," she said.

"Me too," and he gave her a light kiss on the forehead. "What do you wish to do today, Saraste'?"

"I wish to spend as much time as possible lying in my mate's arms," she smiled. "But I expect we will not be allowed that luxury. Are you feeling a need to return to Kthama?"

Oh'Dar sat up. "Yes; is it that obvious? Will you go with me?"

"No. I wish to stay here. Will you be disappointed?"

"Not at all. There are pressing concerns at Kthama, and you will go with me many other times, I am sure. We will figure out how to live in both worlds."

Giving her hip a little pat, Oh'Dar stood up. He pulled on his tunic and stepped outside their shelter to check the weather.

He took a few steps forward and stopped cold.

Carved into the ground, a few feet from their door, was the symbol for *White Wasters*.

Not wanting Acise to see the mark, he quietly scraped it away with his foot. *It has to be Pajackok. He was absent at our bonding ceremony. And now this.*

Oh'Dar stepped back inside, "I am going to see if your parents are awake; take your time getting up."

Honovi and Is'Taqa smiled broadly at seeing him approach. Their fire was already roaring, and the warmth felt good in the cool spring morning. Oh'Dar sat down next to Chief Is'Taqa.

"I was going to return to Kthama. There is much going on there, and I sense that my presence is needed, but—" he paused, looking briefly at Honovi and not wanting to alarm her "—when I stepped outside, someone had drawn the symbol for White Wasters in the ground just a few feet away from our doorway."

Honovi glanced briefly at her partner. "Did Acise see it?"

"No, I scuffed it out. I do not feel right keeping it from her, but I also do not want her alarmed," explained Oh'Dar.

"I will ask if anyone has seen Pajackok," said

Chief Is'Taqa. "He was not at the ceremony yesterday; I know that."

Just then, Noshoba came running up to his father.

"What is wrong?" asked Honovi.

"Pajackok," and he gasped for breath.

"What are you saying? Pajackok *what*?"

"Snana and I were grooming Storm when Pajackok came running up and rode off on his pony. He seemed very angry."

"Did he say anything before he left?"

"Yes, Momma. But I am not supposed to say those words."

Honovi and Is'Taqa looked at each other. "Get as close as you can," his mother directed, "and whisper it to me."

"Tell that white *Soltark;* this is not over."

"What is going on?" Acise's voice startled them; they had not seen her approach.

"From the ground outside our shelter, it looks like someone was in a scuffle. But surely I would have heard if you and Pajackok got into it again?"

"No, I have not seen him—or talked to him— since before our bonding. There was a mark in the ground that I erased so you would not see it," Oh'Dar reluctantly said.

"What kind of mark?" she asked. "Tell me."

"It was the sign for White Wasters," he answered. "I have decided to stay; I am not going to leave you and go to Kthama."

"We will look after Acise, Oh'Dar. Besides, I do not believe the threat is against her," said Is'Taqa.

Oh'Dar looked at his beautiful mate. He was torn.

"Go," she said.

Oh'Dar gently touched her cheek, then acquiesced. He turned to the Chief, "If there is any more trouble, our watchers are still here. Please send word through them, and I will return immediately."

"Do not worry. I know you think that because Acise is part Waschini, the mark was against her too. But I do not believe so. It is yourself you must worry about. I will go and talk to Pajackok's father; he needs to know about this."

Oh'Dar nodded his thanks and was soon on his way back to Kthama. The air was cool, but he kept lapsing into deep thought. *There is no way of knowing where Pajackok is and if he has cooled off at all—and I cannot allow him to catch me off-guard.*

Well before Oh'Dar made it to the Great Entrance, the watchers had alerted Acaraho and Adia that he was on his way back.

His mother came up and hugged him, "Welcome home."

"What is wrong, son?" asked Acaraho, seeing something in Oh'Dar's expression.

Oh'Dar told them of the morning's events.

"I will alert the watchers and ask if any saw him

leave the Brothers' Village. In the meantime, much has happened here, and your mother is waiting to catch you up."

Adia and Oh'Dar went to the Great Chamber and sat down next to Nootau. Adia told them both about the High Council meeting, what she and Urilla Wuti had been told and shared, and the stunned reaction of the High Council members on seeing the burial chamber. Then she added the researchers' news— that it was possible the Leaders had been female, and that the Healers, both male, and female, were allowed to mate and have offspring.

"So, the Overseer is questioning if any of this is true?" Oh'Dar asked.

Adia nodded. "The Overseer's influence is substantial. I do not understand the change. Up until recently, he accepted what was shared—whether from Haan or others. Now he seems to distrust it all. But his suspicion about what we are saying does not seem to be shared by the other Leaders. I hope they can stand strong in their convictions."

"What could have changed, I wonder," Oh'Dar remarked.

They moved on to discuss more personal things, and suddenly Oh'Dar remembered that he and Nootau were due to become big brothers sometime in the future.

"I am sorry, Mama. How is the offspring doing?"

Adia smiled, "He is doing fine."

"It is a male? Father will be so happy."

"Yes, he is. But that does not change how much your father loves both of you," his mother said, looking first at Nootau and then Oh'Dar.

"We know that. Does anyone else know he is a male?" asked Nootau.

"No, we have not shared that."

"When is he due?"

"In about three months, in the warmest part of summer." Adia could strongly feel Nootau and Oh'Dar's happiness for her, though there was something else coming from Nootau that she could not put her finger on. Some time ago, her sensitivity had spiked. She knew from E'ranale that it had something to do with the preparations for opening Kthama Minor and the subsequent release of energy from the vortex.

"How is Tehya? At the ceremony, she looked very thin," observed Oh'Dar.

"She keeps losing weight and is also not sleeping. Do go and see her; I know it would cheer her up. She is sitting over there with Khon'Tor now."

Oh'Dar turned to look, and Tehya waved at him.

Oh'Dar excused himself and walked over. "May I join you?"

Khon'Tor looked up and gestured to a place beside his tiny mate.

Tehya hugged Oh'Dar as he sat down, and he could feel her sharp bones. *Mama is right. This is not good; she was thin to begin with.*

"How is being paired?" asked Khon'Tor.

Oh'Dar grinned, "A great blessing; Acise is wonderful, and we are very happy. But there is some trouble brewing with Pajackok, the brave she was promised to before I returned. It seems that he left me a harsh message on the ground outside of our new shelter."

As they were speaking, one of the watchers, Kahrok, whom Acaraho had demoted from guard, approached their table. Oh'Dar looked him up and down. When they were both offspring, Kahrok had been fond of intimidating Oh'Dar, making it clear that the young Waschini was an Outsider. Kahrok was the exception to the rule of the People's disposition. Neither welcoming nor open, he had always been a bit of a bully. Whether anyone other than Nootau knew of their troubled history together, Oh'Dar did not know.

"We have news, Adik'Tar. I cannot find the High Protector, so I thought I should tell you right away."

"Well, what is it?" barked Khon'Tor.

Kahrok blurted out, "Akar'Tor is alive. We were again checking for any sign of him in the area around the cave where your mate was held captive; we saw Akar'Tor speaking with one of the Sarnonn rebels."

All the color drained from Tehya's face as she leaned away from the table and threw up.

Adia came running over to comfort her just as the Leader lurched at Kahrok, knocking him to the hard rock floor. Khon'Tor began to pummel the watcher, his face contorted with anger.

"Go find your father! Now, Oh'Dar!" shouted Adia.

Oh'Dar immediately took off and Adia wrapped her arms around Tehya as Mapiya hurried over with a damp rag to help clean up.

Hearing the commotion, several guards came running in and immediately tried to pull Khon'Tor off of Kahrok, who was becoming bloodier by the moment. They managed to break Khon'Tor's grasp, at which point Kahrok rolled over gagging and gasping for breath.

More guards poured in, followed by First Guard Awan. They assembled around Khon'Tor, protecting Kahrok from further attack.

In a rage, glaring menacingly at Kahrok, Khon'Tor flipped over one of the nearby tables, shattering the huge slab and sending pieces of rock scattering everywhere.

"*Who is that*?" he demanded, glaring and pointing at Kahrok through the wall of guards.

"It is Kahrok," said Awan, tending to the watcher. "He grew up with Nootau and Oh'Dar. He is of the same age."

"Is he not the second guard who was supposed to be with Tehya when Akar approached her in the Great Chamber?"

"Yes, Adik'Tar. The High Protector demoted him to watcher after that incident," Awan explained.

"Get him out of here!" roared Khon'Tor. "Send him away. To another community, I do not care where. But if I see him here again, *I will kill him*."

Tehya looked up, trying to catch his gaze. "I am alright, Adoeete. Please."

"No, *you are not*," shouted Khon'Tor. "A blind hawk at midnight with no moon could see that you are not. And you will not be until Akar is dead. I know this. This is my fault." Khon'Tor pounded his chest, "*My fault!* I should have killed him when I had the chance."

"Adoeete, please," said Tehya quietly.

"Get him out of here!" ordered Khon'Tor, "*Now!*"

Two of the guards carried Kahrok down a tunnel, out of Khon'Tor's sight.

"Get out of my way—a*ll of you*. I am taking her to our quarters. Adia, come with me," and he scooped up Tehya and stormed off.

Oh'Dar had seen the urgency of the message in his mother's eyes. He had no idea where his father was, but he ran as quickly as he could down the main tunnel to find him.

As he ran past Tar and Nimida in one of the hallways, he called out, "Do you know where my father is?"

"Maybe; earlier he said he would be with Haan

and his people to help them with more of their reorganization," said Tar.

Oh'Dar turned back the way he had come and sprinted off to Kht'shWea to find Acaraho.

Khon'Tor laid Tehya on the oversized softsit that Oh'Dar had made. Adia rinsed out a rag and picked up a gourd of water. She placed it on Tehya's forehead and sat down next to her.

Khon'Tor had not yet gained full control of himself. "Stay with her; I am going to find Acaraho."

Adia looked at Tehya. "Are you feeling better?"

"That was the worst thing I could have done. Khon'Tor is already worried to death because I cannot eat. And now I threw up the little bit I did eat today."

"It is not as if you had a choice. It was just the initial shock of hearing that Akar'Tor is alive. I will bring you some ginger water a little later; I am sure it will stay down. "

"Khon'Tor almost killed that guard. He would have, had Awan and the others not arrived in time."

"He loves you, Tehya. I have never seen him like this; you are his world."

Tehya took a sip of water from the gourd. "If Akar'Tor has joined with the rebel Sarnonn—"

"It does not mean anything. Kayerm is his home; it would be natural that he return there." But even as she said the words, she knew they were not true. Trouble was brewing; she could feel it.

"Adia," said Tehya. "Akar'Tor knows Kthama's location."

They sat together in silence as Adia continued to comfort Tehya.

Oh'Dar found Acaraho and brought him back to Kthama just as Khon'Tor was coming out of the entrance. Haan had followed along.

"Oh'Dar told me. I will address the situation with Kahrok," said Acaraho.

"I have already given Awan orders to get rid of him permanently." Khon'Tor was unmoving.

"Consider it done."

Oh'Dar kept his mouth shut.

"I do not care where you send him; make it clear that he is never to return. If I see him again at Kthama, I will break his neck," snarled the Leader.

"Now that I know Akar is alive—and thanks to Kahrok, so does Tehya," Khon'Tor continued, "I am going to take care of him once and for all."

Haan nodded, not objecting, though he was torn inside. He had raised Akar'Tor as his son, but he also understood Khon'Tor's position. Tehya was innocent. Akar'Tor was anything but, and he presented an ongoing threat to Tehya.

"Haan, I need to know the location of Kayerm.

Akar knows where Kthama is. And we can now assume that the Sarnonn who remain at Kayerm will also know soon enough. We cannot be sure that they will cause trouble, but if Akar has any influence on them, everything I know tells me it will come to that sooner or later."

"It is true. Akar'Tor can lead them here," Haan agreed.

"We are no match for them in numbers, Haan. If there is any chance he is stirring them up against us, or against you, it would be best if we knew about it beforehand."

Haan acquiesced. "I can tell you where Kayerm is located, and you will be able to find it from my directions. But if they have thrown in with Akar'Tor, you stand no chance of taking him."

"If he has stirred them against us, going there would be suicide. You are not thinking clearly," cautioned Acaraho.

Khon'Tor let out a harsh breath. "Alright," he conceded.

Despite his run-in with Tarnor, Akar'Tor had indeed returned to Kayerm. Or at least, to the area surrounding it. The Sarnonn sentries brought the news, and Tarnor sent one of them back to say he had changed his mind and Akar'Tor was welcome at Kayerm.

Accompanied by Tarnor's sentry, Akar'Tor was cautious as he approached his old home. He did not know the reason for the turnaround. *Relax. If they wanted me dead, this huge fellow beside me could already have taken care of that. They have rethought their position. The only explanation is that they want something from me. But what?*

Dorn met Akar'Tor and took him inside Kayerm to meet with Tarnor.

"Welcome home."

"I was not welcome a short while ago; what has changed?" asked Akar'Tor.

"I was hasty. I regret my treatment of you," said Tarnor.

"Not likely. What do you want?"

"Very well. You know the location of Kthama, and we have an interest in that information."

"What is your interest in Kthama? You have Kayerm to yourselves now."

"Your mother—your late mother—seduced the other females with the stories of how much easier life is at Kthama," growled Tarnor. "If she was telling the truth, why should they have the best caves? We are superior to the Akassa; it should belong to us, and we have the might to take it from them."

"What is that information worth? And what is my assurance that after I tell you, you will not have Ar'Rak here dispose of me—since you are *superior* to my kind?"

"I have no quarrel with you. You show us the way

to Kthama. We get Kthama and you get what you want. We promise no harm will come to the little mate of their Leader."

Tehya.

"You must promise no harm to *any* of the females. They are of use to us. The males you can dispatch, I do not care."

"What about your father?"

"If you are talking about Khon'Tor, I would hope to kill him myself. If you are talking about Haan, he has proven he is no longer my father. They are also yours to do with as you wish."

"We cannot guarantee the safety of all the females," said Dorn.

"There is no reason you cannot. They are easily told apart from the males. I get Tehya and a minimum of ten others of my choosing. The rest you can use as you will."

Dorn looked at Tarnor for his agreement.

"If that Akassa wants a collection of females to do with what he will, it is nothing to us," counseled Dorn.

Tarnor scoffed. "Agreed then. Alright. Here is our plan."

After he was alone, Tarnor thought, *You stupid PetaQ; to locate Kthama, I will agree to anything you say. You can have your one night with your precious Tehya; I will give you that. But then, not even Straf'Tor himself could save you—and I will see for myself what is so fascinating about this Tehya.*

Khon'Tor stood in Awan's quarters, unwrapping the huge weapon the First Guard had constructed for him. Setting aside the heavy hide covering, he hefted it, feeling the weight and the balance.

Khon'Tor's eyes met Awan's. Nothing was said. He replaced it in the wrap and handed it to the First Guard.

"I will be back when I have need of it."

Khon'Tor returned to his quarters with Oh'Dar. An idea sprang to mind.

"Oh'Dar. I need your assistance with something. Meet me at your workshop tomorrow at first light."

The young man nodded.

Tehya reached for her mate, and he bent down to be at her level.

"What are you going to do, Adoeete?"

"What I should have done long ago, Saraste'."

The next morning found Oh'Dar and Khon'Tor in the workshop. Khon'Tor explained what he needed. Oh'Dar listened carefully and said he was confident he could make something that would work. "Give me three days and leave the weapon here."

"Be careful of it, Oh'Dar. Its weight is considerable, and it is as deadly as it looks."

"I know. I will be."

Oh'Dar pressed his father into helping him because of the similarities in build between Acaraho and Khon'Tor. And within three days, he accomplished what he had said he would.

Acaraho complimented Oh'Dar on his talent. "We should consider these for all the guards."

The High Protector looked at his reflection on the smooth rock wall. It had been ground down and polished for this very purpose. A strong thick leather band snaked down over his chest and wrapped around his waist. Another band crossed sideways at the top of his chest just under his arms. At the back was a carrier for Khon'Tor's deadly weapon. It was securely encased in a tube fashioned from bamboo and wrapped in the thickest hide available. The combined weight was considerable, yet the contraption made traveling with the weapon safer than it would otherwise be. With one snap to release it, the harness came off and swung forward, bringing the blade around to where it was easily at hand.

"The connection is interesting. Did you invent this or did someone show you how to make it?"

"It is Waschini."

"Khon'Tor will be pleased." Acaraho removed the rest of the harness and hung it from one of the workshop's overhead beams. "Let us get back; Khon'Tor has called for a meeting of the Circle of Counsel."

Oh'Dar shook his head. *I have moved from becoming a healer to designing weaponry garb for warriors. But, as I remember my mother saying, there is a time to wield the blade and a time to lay it down.*

Adia had told Oh'Dar everything she and Urilla Wuti had shared with the High Council. This time, Haan sat with them as part of Khon'Tor's inner circle. Tehya was not up to attending, and was in the Leader's Quarters being cared for by Nimida with instructions to try to get her to eat, and to interrupt should her condition become worse.

Khon'Tor spoke first. "I called this meeting because of the certainty that the Sarnonn who remain at Kayerm know where to find Kthama."

"We believe Kayerm is located not far from the cave where Akar'Tor held Tehya captive," explained Acaraho, "but putting watchers into the area would alert the leaders of their group that we suspect they are up to something. If they are going to attack us, it is better that they think we are unprepared and unawares."

"But we do have some watchers already placed in

strategic locations closer to home to observe any movement toward Kthama. They have been alerted and are on high watch status," Awan added.

"Haan, do you have any idea when they would try to take Kthama, if that is what they are up to?"

"I do not, Khon'Tor. Though I suspect they would try sooner as opposed to later. They know that my people and I are displaced. Whether or not it has occurred to them that you would give us Kthama Minor, I do not know. But there is no benefit to them in waiting. In their position, I would not. But we do not know that an attack is what they intend," he added.

"We have to assume it is," said Khon'Tor. "There is no doubt in my mind that Akar is not done with his desire to lead Kthama. Nor done with his intentions toward Tehya."

"Then you must plan and prepare for the worst," conceded Haan. "There is only one direction from which they could approach, and your watchers will see them well before they could get near to Kthama. No doubt they would come in force, in which case you are no match for them. You will be able to take out some of them, but in the final count, Khon'Tor, *Kthama will fall.*"

"Even with your help?" he asked.

"Yes. Do not doubt that we will stand with you or that we will do all we can to defend Kthama and Kht'shWea. But they outnumber us considerably. "

Silence.

"Khon'Tor, we need to move all the females, elderly, and offspring," said Acaraho.

Khon'Tor nodded. "And the record-keepers. They are irreplaceable. What about the Sarnonn females, Haan?"

"I will leave it to them. Those with new offling perhaps, certainly Haaka and Kalli," Haan answered. "But it will cut our numbers in half. Many of them would choose to stay and fight. If we lose, their lives with the rebels will not be pleasant for their part in supporting the Akassa and me."

"All the People's females," Acaraho reiterated, looking at Khon'Tor.

Khon'Tor knew what he meant. No doubt, Akar'-Tor's intention was possession of Tehya. Neither Adia nor Tehya were in good condition to be moved quickly, and they would not go quietly.

"I do not know how long they will have to be away, so we must ask Harak'Sar or Lesharo'Mok to take everyone in. But the Deep Valley and the Far High Hills can be accessed from the Mother Stream, so the People's first line of defense is Kthama. It is crucial to shore up our defenses here, and I am sure Harak'Sar and Lesharo'Mok will both send for their males to stand with us."

"We will start sending our vulnerable away as soon as we have permission from the other Leaders," declared Khon'Tor. "I will seek out both of them now. That is all."

"Khon'Tor, wait. What about the Brothers' village?" interrupted Oh'Dar.

"They will not harm the Brothers," said Haan. "The Mothoc were the keepers of the Brothers, and enough harm has been done to them. There is no quarrel there, and they will not be touched."

Once alone, Adia took Acaraho's arm.

"I am not leaving you. Tehya will not go either."

"It is not optional. You will leave, and so will Tehya. That is the end of it."

"You cannot make me; I outrank you."

"You can try that, Healer, but it will be to no avail. In times of crisis, I outrank you, and you know it."

She glared at him.

"Saraste', I cannot protect you and fight the Sarnonn. Your presence here will be a liability. For the males to have any chance of survival, we need all our focus on preparing for the attack. If or when it comes, knowing you are somewhere else, safe and protected, that is the best gift you can give me for my chance of survival. And it is the same for Khon'Tor with Tehya. You must help her understand this too. We also know that she is at risk where Akar'Tor is concerned."

Tears ran down Adia's cheeks. "I cannot lose you. Neither can our son. Our life together has just begun."

"I promise you that with all my strength, I will fight to live. And if there is any way to do so, I will live to come home to your arms."

Preparations began after the High Council was appraised of the situation. The other Leaders agreed unequivocally to take in the record keepers, females, Elders, and offspring. Messengers were sent, and on their Leaders' orders, the communities were sending males to support the defense of Kthama. The Far High Hills and the Deep Valley had committed to making as many spears as possible to send with their males.

Khon'Tor then met with the High Council members. "Once our defenseless are safely away from Kthama, we will post reinforcements at several points along the Mother Stream. If worse comes to worst and our forces fail, we will destroy the tunnel."

The other Leaders looked at each other.

"Once done, there will be no way to open it again," said the Overseer, stating the obvious.

Destroying the tunnel would block the underground passage from Kthama to their communities forever. But it would also mean that the Sarnonn would have no easy way of discovering and reaching the other locations.

"Only as a last resort, should Kthama fall," said Khon'Tor. "We will use whatever time we have to strategize a defense. Though Haan is not positive about the outcome—even with his help—we may be able to reduce the numbers sufficient to allow the other communities to wage a winning counter-attack. The rebels' goal would be Kthama, which makes their location known, should they prevail. We can only hope that if they capture Kthama, they will be satisfied with that."

Khon'Tor braced himself for the most difficult speech he had ever had to give. He stepped forward, his Leader's Staff in his hand. The High Protector, First Guard Awan, the two Healers, Tehya, Nadiwani, Mapiya, and Haan stood with him, while the High Council members stood at the back of the room. Tension filled the air even though the community did not know what to expect.

"People of the High Rocks. Today, I come bearing difficult news. Though we have made a peaceful alliance with Haan and his people, there is a rebel Sarnonn element from which we believe trouble is coming. In an abundance of caution, I am ordering the urgent evacuation of many from Kthama. The Leaders of the Far High Hills and the Deep Valley have offered sanctuary in their communities. As I speak, they are making arrange-ments to receive all of our elderly, infirm, females, and offspring. They will also be sending many of their males to stand with ours in defense of Kthama."

Khon'Tor waited for the anxious talking to die down. "I know this is alarming. It is a precaution, but one I do not take lightly. I do not know how long you will be away from home. Rest assured that Haan has pledged his people, our neighbors, to stand with us in what we believe will be an attempt to take Kthama. Now you understand why I am ordering you to vacate our home."

As prearranged, Haan stepped forward to address the crowd.

"People of Kthama. I deeply regret that our coming to the High Rocks has resulted in this threat to you and your home. My people and I will be standing with your Adik'Tar and your males to defend Kthama. We will do everything in our power to protect you in hopes that you will be able to be reunited with your loved ones and resume your lives here."

Khon'Tor resumed, "It will be several days' journey, so only pack what you cannot bear the possibility of losing. We will have guards posted along the Mother Stream, ready to carry the news to you while you are with your host communities. We have never faced an attack of this kind, but we will fight for you and Kthama with everything we have. May the Great Spirit show us favor. That is all."

Khon'Tor brought the Leader's Staff down with a resounding crack.

The Leaders stayed in the Great Chamber for some time, talking to the most rattled and trying to comfort them.

Over the next few days, everyone leaving packed their essentials and prepared for the possibility of never being able to return. Extra foodstuffs were included where they could be—mostly dried nuts and fruits, which would transport well. Many of the females did not want to leave, but their mates insisted on it, understanding that to stay would be suicide, risking capture or death if Kthama fell. Loved ones grouped tensely together with tearful embraces and last parting words. The haven that had been their home was being ripped away.

The Overseer and the other High Council members had gone ahead to the Far High Hills, even though it was farther than the first large community, the Deep Valley. It would be safer because of its greater distance from Kthama. As long as possible, the leadership would stay together because time would be of the essence for decision making—unless more pressing circumstances demanded they scatter back to their communities.

Khon'Tor, Acaraho, Nootau, and Oh'Dar stood at the entrance to the Mother Stream, with Tehya, Adia, and Urilla Wuti. First Guard Awan, Akule, and several of the other guards stood ready to escort the

Second and Third Rank females to safety. Nadiwani had already left in the same group as Nimida, Mapiya, Pakuna, and some others. Because of their condition, Adia being nearly full-term and Tehya being so frail, their going would be as slow as with the elderly.

The Leaders had decided that the Healers would accompany Tehya. Khon'Tor was relieved that she would be at the Far High Hills with her parents and that she and Arismae would be as safe there as could be.

Tears streamed down Tehya's face as she clung to Khon'Tor. "Please do not make me leave."

"There is no more discussion. You and Arismae must go. We have been through this."

"I cannot imagine life without you."

"Nor can I without you." Despite the presence of the others, Khon'Tor was no longer going to hold back out of pride. He wrapped her in his arms and buried his face in her hair. "You are everything to me, Saraste'," he whispered to her. "If there is any way in krell, I will survive." He took her face gently in his hands and looked deep in her eyes, "Please promise you will safely wait for me at the Far High Hills."

Tehya sobbed openly, and Khon'Tor pulled her closer while Kweeuu waited patiently at her feet.

"Why can you not come with us? There is no benefit to staying here, in sacrificing yourself," she said.

"We have also been through this. I must stand

with those of our males who are staying and those from the other communities who intend to fight with us. We also cannot let the Sarnonn fight this on their own. Only a coward without honor would save himself and abandon everyone else to fight alone."

"To die alone, you mean," she said. Khon'Tor pulled her even more tightly to him.

"Haan could be right," he said softly. "In the end, Kthama may fall. But together, we will do significant damage. And however many we can take out will leave that many less for any attacks against the other communities. There is no higher honor than defending that which you love most."

Adia and Acaraho were off to the side, also saying their goodbyes.

"This cannot be happening. Ever since I was chosen to be a Healer, I never dreamed I would have a chance to be paired, to have what I envied all the other females for. And now not only that, but more. Now I bear your offspring. He cannot grow up without you. He must know what a wonderful Leader and what a wonderful soul his father is. He must benefit from your love and guidance, just as Oh'Dar and Nootau have. You must live. You must."

"I will use everything within my power to survive. I promise you that."

Oh'Dar watched his parents, giving them their time together. When they separated, he went over to them.

Both put their arms around their son and hugged him.

"No matter what. Live your life. Enjoy your life, Oh'Dar. If I do not survive, know that I died blessed to have lived long enough to see you paired, and have a chance at the kind of happiness your mother and I have shared. We are proud of you, Oh'Dar, and we love you with all our hearts."

"No, I am staying to fight with you," Oh'Dar said calmly.

"Son, I appreciate your willingness, but it would be too risky. Acise needs you, as do the Brothers and the People. If we are not successful, word will make it to the Brothers' village. If I do not survive, I am counting on you and your brother to find your mother and take care of her and the offspring. But be careful not to travel too soon. Remember that anger passes slowly, and you must not risk any of the Sarnonn following you or anyone else. Once the rebels have what they want, they will most likely be satisfied."

Oh'Dar reluctantly nodded, doing his best to control his emotion.

Acaraho turned to Nootau. "My son, you do not realize how strong you are. Find your place here among the People. Be aware that it may not be what you think it is. Remember everything I taught you. Above all, influence others with wisdom, forbearance, gentleness. But never forget there comes a time to stand your ground—true leadership guides with both a soft and a hard hand. And I pray that you someday find the same happiness with someone as I have found with your mother."

"Why are you saying this, father? *You are coming back.* Besides, I am no Leader, and I wish to stay and fight with you."

"As far as being a Leader is concerned, perhaps not in title, but I have watched you grow all these years, and others look up to you and respect you. Not everyone who has a title is a leader, and not everyone who is a leader has a title," he replied. "I cannot have you here for the same reason as the other younger males who have not produced offspring cannot be here. We cannot lose all the male bloodlines from Kthama, and those of us staying to fight will not be able effectively to do so if distracted by what is happening to our sons."

Then Acaraho embraced Nootau, "Never forget how much we love you." And he turned back to the others.

Hugs were shared all around, and then it was time to go. As Tehya hugged Oh'Dar, she whispered in his ear, "Do not worry, I will keep Kweeuu safe."

Awan had been watching the other guards saying goodbye to their loved ones and suddenly wished he had loved ones of his own.

Despite the seriousness, there were reluctant smiles at Kweeuu, outfitted with the carrying basket and harness that Oh'Dar had made for him long ago, now adjusted for his full-grown weight. In it were his food and water bowls, and the hide bear toy made for him years earlier.

The males stood and watched them disappear around the corner. Everything that mattered. Everything worth fighting for. Everything worth dying for. They turned and looked at each other.

"Now we wait," said Khon'Tor.

They did not have to wait long.

The Sarnonn rebels had not delayed in making their plans to take Kthama. Though they outpowered the People, they wanted every advantage possible, and they counted on the element of surprise as one.

All in all, there were nearly two hundred Sarnonn males. The females and offling were to stay behind with a small complement of guards. Tarnor was confident that the People would not be stupid enough to attack them, even if Haan had revealed Kayerm's location.

Dorn had instructed the males to construct extra-long spears from thick tree branches. Though the Sarnonn could easily overpower the People, the additional length of the spear extended their reach, and the heft of the spears would be efficient in taking out several of the People with one swing.

The rebels knew they had the advantage after dark. They knew from experience with Hakani and Akar'Tor that the People had weaker low-light vision than the Sarnonn. However, a negative was that they were dependent on Akar'Tor to show the way; he had not revealed the location because he was holding the information back as leverage.

Akar'Tor was not foolish enough to trust Tarnor or Dorn. He hoped his logic in convincing them to keep the People's females alive had been sufficient, but regardless, victory belonged to the Sassen. Once the battle had begun, his first and primary target was Tehya. With all the commotion that would ensue, he doubted he had any chance of killing Khon'Tor himself. But if he could witness Khon'Tor's death, that would be a bonus, but one for which he would not compromise any chance to recapture Tehya. His body quickened at the thought of having her to himself; this time, nothing would keep him from claiming her.

The calls of night birds sweetened the cool air. Overhead in the clear sky, a crescent moon cast a dim light over the sprawling landscape below Kthama's entrance. The watchers were on high alert, and Khon'Tor, Acaraho, and many of the others were sleeping in the Great Entrance lest precious time be lost. The two fastest runners were ready to travel two different routes to carry the message to Haan should the Sarnonn threat be spotted.

Through the relative darkness, the Sarnonn band approached Kthama. They knew the People would be alerted well before they reached it, and having Akar'Tor in the lead slowed everyone down. But it did not matter. Dorn and Tarnor were confident of their success, no matter how long it took them to get there, and no matter how much warning the People had.

It was likely that the Sarnonn renegades would strike under cover of darkness, and it was a long time since either Khon'Tor or Acaraho had gotten a sound night's sleep. They were ever-alert, and each night, they knew that this could be that of the Sarnonn attack.

Finally, it came. The Leaders rose quickly and assembled with a third of the guards who were taking the forward position with them. Others were ready to approach from the sides, strategizing that some element of surprise might offset the greater brute strength of Sarnonn.

Khon'Tor and his band exited the mouth of Kthama with some time before the rebels would arrive. The watchers had been ordered to stay in their posts, no matter what happened. If it appeared inevitable that Kthama would be taken, they were to abandon their places and save themselves.

It was time. Khon'Tor, Acaraho, Awan, and the others prepared to make their descent, not willing to meet the Sarnonn on the steep and rocky paths that led to the Great Entrance. Their best chance of survival would be to have sure footing on solid ground.

First Guard Awan now stood with the Leader and the High Protector. "The runners will have reached Haan by now," said Acaraho.

"Commander," began Awan.

Acaraho turned to him. "This is not the time for formalities, brother of mine. I am both sorry and glad that you are with me at this time. I will always be grateful to your father and mother for taking me in. We have traveled our journey together, and I would not be half the person you say I am, were it not for your family's love and care." Acaraho placed his hand on Awan's shoulder, and Awan returned the gesture.

"It has been an honor," said the First Guard, and they briefly embraced.

Acaraho turned to Khon'Tor.

"If I have to die, there is some comfort in falling by your side. I know we have had our share of troubles. And there are some things that even though I may understand, I can never forgive you for. But now, at this moment, I call you friend."

Khon'Tor briefly closed his eyes. "You have never

wavered in your service or your loyalty. You have given me far more respect and many chances more than I deserve. I am equally proud to call you friend."

They stood a moment in silence before Acaraho continued. "It is unlikely that both of us will survive. No doubt, we will be the first target. If one of us survives, he must let the other's mate know that she was the last thought on her mate's mind and that his love for her lives on past the last beating of his heart," said Acaraho.

Khon'Tor nodded.

"It is time," said Awan, pointing.

Off in the distance, a large wall of bodies marched through the dark toward them.

They reached the bottom of the path, their hearts pounding in their chests.

"Where are Haan and his people? They should be here by now," said Acaraho looking around. "The other males are waiting for our signal to attack, but we agreed we would wait for Haan and his people to show up first."

Khon'Tor had a sick feeling in his stomach. *Where are they? No. Surely Haan would not set us up? Please do not tell me that in the end, I have failed everyone who depended on me, and am to die a fool.*

The wall of Sarnonn had crossed the meadow and reached paths below the seat of Kthama. Khon'-Tor, Acaraho, and the other males stood ready.

Within a few moments, the army of giants would be upon them.

"Haan is not coming. We have been betrayed," said Acaraho.

"We can still try to take out their leaders, Dorn and Tarnor, as planned—if, without Haan's help, we can pick them out. As he said, eliminating them might be enough for the others to lose their resolve."

"Agreed. So let us not die standing here like helpless fawns, inevitably to be slaughtered. Are you ready?"

Acaraho nodded, and they raised their spears.

All the males present released ear-splitting screamcalls and charged at the Sarnonn, who stopped their forward movement and stood still—a solid dark wall of death waiting motionless for the opposition to reach them. There was no hurry; the rebels were assured of the eventual outcome.

Just as the People were within several strides of the Sarnonn, a crack of thunder split the silence, louder than anything ever heard before on Etera. Everyone startled, then involuntarily froze and turned to look overhead.

A brilliant tunnel of white light shot up from the meadow above Kthama, turning the dark night to day. All of them, Sarnonn and People alike, covered their eyes against the blinding brightness.

Every night sound was silenced, and time seemed to stop her forward movement.

Slowly, the funnel of light turned unnaturally,

curved down, and settled in the space that remained between the two factions. The blazing column of light crackled and sparked like lightning, and an acrid smell of burning grass and singed earth assaulted their nostrils.

All shaded their eyes and stepped back, widening the gap between them.

As their sight adjusted, Haan and his Sarnonn followers could be seen emerging from the woods to the north. In a single line and moving as one, just as they had when opening Kthama Minor, they marched between the two regiments and circled the light. When they were evenly spaced, they turned their backs to the beam and came to a stop.

A loud voice thundered through, easily heard over the snapping and spitting of the light. Speaking in the same ancient language used by Haan and his people to open Kthama Minor, the voice boomed, "The first Sarnonn who moves toward the Akassa forfeits his life and those of all the others." Then, out of the column of brightness, a figure started forming before them, huge, looming, larger than life.

Acaraho and Khon'Tor exchanged fleeting glances. Though the language was as unrecognizable as before, this time, they could understand everything.

The Sarnonn were staring in awe as the figure became clearer. It was a Mothoc, one of the Fathers, though, from the dark coat, it was not Moc'Tor.

"I have waited all this time—and for what?"

Somehow they knew; they all knew. It was Straf'Tor himself, father of the Sarnonn. Understanding who was addressing them, the entire complement of rebel Sarnonn fell straight to its knees, spears dropping to the ground.

"For you to turn against your brothers the Akassa at the first chance?" continued the Mothoc giant, addressing Tarnor and his contingent. "Is this what Moc'Tor and the rest of us sacrificed ourselves for? So that you would, in the end, in your ignorance and hatred, destroy your only hope, taking with it all hope for Etera herself?

"We gave you the Rah-hora. We protected you from each other so that together you might have a chance to create the future of your making. To save yourselves and the rest of creation."

There was a pause. "Step forward, Tarnor of Kayerm," boomed Straf'Tor's voice.

Tarnor was frozen with terror and unable to move. His mind was reeling. *How is it possible?* Yet there was no mistaking the fact that this was indeed Straf'Tor himself standing before them.

"Straf'Tor, Adik'Tar," he said as he stumbled to his feet and stepped forward. "How is this possible?"

"How is it possible that I am standing before you now? We told you we would be watching. And that when the shadow of Wrak-Ayya fell, the true test would begin. A test you have failed miserably, and not only failed yourself but with others whom you have turned to your evil intentions. The future is not written. All is not *yet* lost. But what have you done? You have plotted division from the first moment you learned of the Sassen's contact with the Akassa. And now, even worse, you come to annihilate them. I stand as your judge, and I decree, Tarnor, that there is no place for your influence in the future that can still come to pass."

And with that, Straf'Tor's apparition passed through the circle of Haan's people as if they were not there. He reached out and snapped Tarnor's neck as easily as one might break a tiny dry twig between one's thumb and finger.

Tarnor's lifeless body crumpled to the ground, illuminated by the light that surrounded Straf'Tor.

The Mothoc legend took another step toward the Sarnonn, most of whom now cowered where they knelt, though some scrambled to put more distance between them and the huge, menacing figure.

"The Healer of the Akassa has already brought to the High Council the message from Moc'Tor's mate, E'ranale. So I bring you the same message; the division between the Sassen and the Akassa was necessary. Your bloodline was to be kept as pure as possible, so there would be enough of the Mothoc blood to perform the Ror'Eckrah when it came time to open Kthama Minor. It was also for the protection of the Akassa—for which you have just so perfectly proven the need. In turn, your existence was kept from the Akassa lest, in their ignorance, they influence you to divert the Mothoc blood further. Without cooperation between the Sassen and the Akassa, the heart of Etera will sicken and die. Together, you have a chance to save Etera—and each other—but you must first make peace with the Akassa.

"And now, as a consequence of your hostilities, you must accept their rule over you. You are no longer their equals, nor are you the equals of the Sassen standing with Haan, son of 'Tor. You are relegated to be their protectors, and you will accept Haan's rule over you. This is your last chance and your last warning. Accept your status and your fate. We will be watching; should any of the Akassa be harmed, make no mistake, I will return and kill every one of you just as easily as I have Tarnor."

Then Straf'Tor turned to address the Akassa.

"Not one of you need fear me; we know the Akassa are not the aggressors. You also have no need to fear Tarnor's band any longer, so go and retrieve your loved ones."

Straf'Tor stepped forward and stopped before Khon'Tor, illuminating the Leader's entire form.

"You, son of Moc'Tor, you know what you must do. You have known for some time. There are hard choices ahead for you, but the fate of your very soul demands that you face them. As for Akar'Tor, the seed of your loins—though he is as guilty in this abomination as Tarnor, I will leave him for you to deal with."

Then he addressed Acaraho, "And you, my son. There are also challenges awaiting you. Find the strength to take your rightful place; step out from the shadows of those who have gone before."

Straf'Tor took one last slow look around, making eye contact with each person there. Then he raised his hand and announced, "I leave you to the future of your making."

And with that, the apparition wavered and disappeared. With a huge crack, the light that had streamed out from the meadow above Kht'shWea disappeared as dramatically as it had come.

Nobody moved. Neither Sarnonn nor People.

Tarnor's body lay crumpled and motionless on the ground.

Then Haan's group slowly started to regain their individuality. Not as exhausted as after the opening of Kht'shWea, they remained standing and began milling quietly about.

Haan came out of his trance and approached Tarnor and the other rebel Sarnonn, on his way making a point of stepping over Tarnor's body.

"Dorn, Straf'Tor has spoken, and now so shall I. If your hearts have truly changed, you are welcome to join us. The Akassa have given us Kthama Minor. In time, I hope we will be able to reunite our people and discover together the future of our making, as brothers and protectors of the Akassa."

Dorn nodded solemnly. He turned to his people and shouted into the air, still acrid with smoke.

"Hear me, sons of Straf'Tor. We will return to Kayerm in peace; the time of division is over. Let there be no further talk of hostilities against the Akassa. Anyone speaking of such things will be killed on the spot, on my order. You heard Straf'Tor; he will destroy us all. Now, rise and return to Kayerm. Tomorrow is a new day."

Khon'Tor and his people stood watching as the Sarnonn rose from their knees, brushed themselves off, and wearily turned back the way they had come. There was little talk among them, as their minds and souls were reeling from what they have just experienced.

"Dorn, return here alone in the morning so we can talk," said Haan. "I will have an escort waiting for you."

Dorn turned to leave, then stopped and addressed Khon'Tor and all the males who stood with him.

"For what it is worth, we were wrong. I was wrong. I was no better than Tarnor; I do not know why Straf'Tor let me live."

"Your people need someone to lead them into peace between us," answered Haan. "Apparently, to that end, Straf'Tor saw potential in you."

Dorn shook his head, then turned and followed the others. They left the ground strewn with spears.

Haan turned to Khon'Tor.

"You were late," said Khon'Tor sternly.

"My apologies, Adik'Tar 'Tor. But we were not too late, and that is what matters," replied Haan, smiling.

Acaraho and the others broke into laughter, the strain of the past few hours finally shattered.

Exhausted and elated, they were not sure what to do.

Haan broke the silence. "Tomorrow, I will meet with Dorn and discuss the peaceful coexistence of our people. My ultimate hope is to reunite us at Kht'shWea. You do not need to fear them, Khon'Tor. As you know, it was Straf'Tor himself who stood before them. Just as Moc'Tor's people stayed at Kthama, it was Straf'Tor's who left Kthama for Kayerm. But we had no forewarning of what has just happened. As I was bringing my males down to back you up, the twelve Guardians took their places at the stones. What guided them to do so, I do not know. But once they were in position, the Ror'Eckrah came over us."

"We have much to think about and much to discuss. Straf'Tor said it is safe to fetch the others—" said Khon'Tor.

"It is safe; Tarnor's followers no longer pose any threat. But for your peace of mind, we will not drop our guard. And now and forever, we will stand ready to protect both Kthama and Kht'shWea."

As they headed home together, the thoughts of both Khon'Tor and Acaraho ran in the same vein.

Where is Akar'Tor?

From the highest treetop, Akar'Tor had seen it all. As the renegades entered the battle zone, he had slipped away and climbed to safety. He now clung to the branches, stunned.

Certain victory had been plucked from his hand by the supernatural intervention of a dead Mothoc. *The cowards. They did not even try to fight. They betrayed me, and now I will never recover Tehya.*

CHAPTER 4

Up in the meadow above Kht'shWea, the twelve silver Sarnonn Guardians stepped forward from their places in front of the crystal monoliths.

"That was Straf'Tor himself," said Thord.

"How did we do it?" asked one of the others.

"I do not know," replied Thord. "I wonder what other powers we have. I can feel great strength coursing through me, and I have more energy than I ever remember having—even as an offling."

"Whatever has happened to us, it is good," answered Lellaach, Thord's mate.

The others all nodded.

Lellaach continued, "It is as if a well of life force exists below us, far below this meadow and both cave systems. And somehow, we are tapped into it."

Thord put his arm around her, "Perhaps in time, we will be told what all this means. But in the meantime, let us enjoy this wonderful gift of vitality and happiness. And it seems we will be in the forefront whatever wonders may yet manifest."

The others nodded in agreement, and in their pairs, made their way toward Kht'shWea.

When they arrived, Haan was still up waiting for them and watched them enter Kht'shWea's Great Entrance. He was tired and might be mistaken, but he thought there was a faint glow about them.

"Well, Adik'Tar, that was interesting," said Thord, who had become the unofficial Leader of the six males. "These are exciting times. We are blessed among males to be part of them."

"From your positions, could you hear what Straf'Tor said?" asked Haan. "It was so far away. And what prompted you to take your places at the stones?"

"It was a pull. An irresistible pull. We knew we were supposed to start down to the valley, but something drew us to our places. And yes, we could hear what was happening; we heard and saw everything."

Haan waited, hoping that Thord would explain more.

Lellaach spoke up. "Yes, it was as if we *were* Straf'Tor. We saw it through his eyes—yet we also saw it through yours and those of the Akassa. As if we were somehow everywhere at once.

At that point, having heard all the others return, Haaka arrived with Kalli on her hip to find Haan.

"Come to bed, please. You look exhausted." Haaka took Haan's hand and tugged on it.

He nodded. "We will meet in the morning. I need to share with everyone the messages given by E'ranale to the Akassa Healers."

They all shook their heads. *First Straf'Tor, and now E'ranale?*

The group disbanded, no one sure they *would* be able to sleep after the excitement of the night's events.

Haan lay on the sleeping mat, waiting for the release of sleep. *I know now who destroyed the first area we prepared. It was Straf'Tor himself. Only a Mothoc would have had the strength to shatter the generator stones and scatter them about. Entire trees were uprooted. Had he not forced us to find another location, the life force released when we joined in Ror'Eckrah would have created the same blossoming there and on the path to the Healer's stone—leading Tarnor's gang directly to Kthama well before we could have been ready to face them.* He reflected that somehow the Mothoc's reach extended into Etera's realm even without the Ror'Eckrah.

Sitting on the ground in the Circle of Counsel meeting room, their backs propped up against the wall, Khon'Tor, Awan, and Acaraho had only dozed for what remained of the night. Despite their exhaustion, there was too much to think over. They had looked death in the face and survived. Together.

Khon'Tor was reflecting on what the figure of Straf'Tor had said to him, *"You, son of Moc'Tor, you know what you must do. You have known for some time. There are hard choices ahead for you, but the fate of your very soul demands that you face them."*

And Khon'Tor knew exactly what he meant.

Acaraho stirred and opened his eyes to see Khon'Tor still a few feet away. "I did not expect to see this day," he said, stretching his arms overhead.

"Nor did I."

"Shall we send for the females and the others?"

"Not yet. I wish instead to travel to the Far High Hills, and you must come with me. There is something I need to do. Something I should have done a long time ago."

Acaraho looked puzzled but did not ask. "I can be ready when you are," he said. "But I would like to tell Haan myself that we are leaving. When will we be returning to Kthama?"

"I cannot answer that," said Khon'Tor quietly.

Knowing that Haan and his people were watching over Kthama, they agreed that First Guard Awan and a few males from Kthama, as well as the males who had come from the other communities, would follow on behind them to the Far High Hills.

Many would be able to bear witness to others of the amazing events they had witnessed the night before.

Before the morning passed, the two males had each packed supplies and set out along the Mother Stream toward the Far High Hills.

They walked mostly in silence, each lost in his own thoughts. As they traveled, they passed the guards Acaraho had staged at strategic points. After updating them, the High Protector sent one on ahead to let the other communities know that Kthama was secure and told the others to stay at their posts until they received word to return to Kthama. They also left foodstuffs with some whose supplies were running low.

After a brief stop at the Deep Valley to share the good news, finally, they came to the exit from the Mother Stream, which led them back above ground to Amara, the dwelling of the People of the Far High Hills. Harak'Sar's guard immediately recognized Khon'Tor and ran ahead to send word he was approaching. By the time they got to the entrance, a crowd had assembled.

As Khon'Tor stepped into the clear, a small figure bolted out and flung itself at him. He opened his arms to embrace his beloved Tehya, now once again safe in his arms. She clung to him, arms around his neck and legs wrapped as far around him as they could reach, as he held her firmly.

Within seconds, Adia also broke from the crowd and headed straight to Acaraho. He leaned down to embrace her gently, taking care not to put any pressure on her bulging middle.

"By the Mother, my prayers have been answered," said Urilla Wuti.

Harak'Sar approached the High Rocks Leaders. "I truly did not expect to see you ever again, Khon'Tor, Commander."

"Nor did we expect to see you," answered Khon'Tor. "By a miracle, we suffered no casualties. Everyone is safe and healthy."

Harak'Sar turned to the crowd and raising his voice, repeated what Khon'Tor had said.

A spontaneous cheer arose from the People, accompanied by much hugging and laughing.

The Leader continued, "Come, let us get you settled. I have a thousand questions, which I am sure you will answer in time, but you both no doubt need to rest and have some quiet time with your families."

Once inside, Adia started sobbing.

Acaraho pulled her to him and held her close, stroking her hair. He let her cry out her release, knowing the stress on her had been terrible.

"I feared I had lost you."

"I do not know where to start. About what happened. Amazing things, unbelievable things. If the Overseer had trouble believing all this before, he will never accept what we are to tell him next."

"There will be time for all of that. Tell me only when you wish, if you are up to it. Perhaps now you should just rest, my love."

Suddenly, all the exhaustion Acaraho had been pushing aside came crashing down. "Yes. You are right. Come here to me; we will rest together." They moved to the sleeping mat, and Acaraho protectively wrapped himself around Adia. Within moments she could tell he was sound asleep. Until exhaustion won, she lay there and thanked the Great Mother with all her heart and soul that her beloved had been safely returned.

Tehya stepped inside and motioned for the guards to close the door behind them.

Khon'Tor looked around the room. It was much smaller than their quarters at Kthama, but in a way, charming—somehow comforting. "Where is Arismae?"

Tehya said, "She is with my parents at the moment."

Khon'Tor continued sweeping the room and looked over at the sleeping area. He noticed the white feather he had given Tehya in what seemed like a lifetime ago. He went over and picked it up. "You still have it."

"Of course," she whispered. "I will never let go of it, any more than I will ever let go of you."

He set the feather back down in its place next to the first necklace he had given Tehya, suddenly remembering the second Oh'Dar had made but which she had not yet been given. He turned back and looked her up and down carefully, then picked up her hands and examined them. He brushed a lock of hair from her forehead. He noticed the dark circles under her eyes had faded a bit, and perhaps she had put on a little weight.

"Have you been sleeping? You look a bit better to me." His hand caressed her face.

"Despite the unbearable heartache of thinking I had lost you, I have been sleeping and eating better."

Khon'Tor was relieved to hear this and especially glad that she was getting rest. *But what will happen now that I am back alongside her at night?*

"You must tell me what happened. By what miracle are you standing here with me now?"

"I will tell you; I will tell you everything, but at this moment I want only to be with you. I thought I might never see you again."

Tehya leaned up on her tiptoes and kissed him gently, then took his hand and led him to the sleeping mat.

She sat and pulled him down beside her. Then

she stretched out, "Please, come. I have missed you so."

Khon'Tor sat down next to her, unsure of what she was asking. He ached to take her, to be buried inside her, but had promised he would wait until she was ready.

He took one of her feet in his hands and massaged it, giving each little toe its due. She closed her eyes and murmured how good it felt. After a moment, she shifted her position a little. And she did so, her wrap slipped. The brief glimpse made him catch his breath, but he continued to rub her feet, changing between one then the other. Then he moved up her calves, enjoying the sounds of pleasure she was making.

He had vowed to wait until she was ready. Between her distractions as a new mother, and now this nightmare, he did not want to rush her. But oh, how he wished she would give him a sign.

As he massaged her legs, she moved again—giving him a better view. Is she doing this on purpose? His heart rate increased. *Is she teasing me? Inviting me?*

He moved his hands up higher, to her thighs, unable to take his eyes off her. He gently kneaded them, careful not to hurt her. Finally, when she took his left hand and placed it exactly on the area he had been longing to touch, there was no mistaking her intentions.

He did his best to pleasure her, feeling her desire

for him growing under his attention. He caressed her gently, circling and teasing, grateful for the Ashwea Tare that taught the males how to patiently please their females.

Tehya opened her eyes and slowly sat up, guiding him to lie down next to her. Once he had done so, she crawled up on top of him. To his surprise, she took him into herself. Absolved for the moment of the responsibility to please her, he closed his eyes at the sheer pleasure. After a moment, he opened them and focused on the view of this beautiful female moving over him. Knowing that she was shifting her body as it suited her, he let her use him to please herself. Then he reached up and undid the front of her tie, the knot coming loose in one smooth motion. He helped her slip off her top so he could have a full view of her pink-tipped, full mounds. As she moved faster, he placed his hands on her hips to help steady her, supporting her rhythm but not guiding it. She closed her eyes in pleasure, which let him study her all the more intently. The view of her straddling him, sheathing him and grinding herself into him as she wanted was driving him close to the edge. He willed his body to hold back and not spend his seed before she finished but was not sure he could hold out. It had been some time since either had experienced release. "Tehya," he whispered. She increased the force of her movements, leaning forward and bracing herself with her hands on his chest, her long hair gently flogging him as she rocked back and forth with increasing fervor. "I can—not—" he said, and then he felt her tighten around him and watched ecstasy cover her face. She moaned in delight, arched her back, and pressed harder against him, burying him more deeply into her than he would ever have dared. Khon'Tor could hold back no longer and emptied into her, losing himself in the exquisite pleasure. Never one to call out, his last shred of control broke, he surprised her with a deep moan of release.

Tehya collapsed onto his chest, and silently they lay together for a moment, she nestled into her favorite spot against him. After a few moments, he flipped her around and protectively curled himself around her, kissing her neck and smoothing the hair from her forehead, saying how much he loved her.

As he cuddled her, Straf'Tor's words came back to him. Haunting him, robbing him of the peace of the moment.

"Saraste', there are things I must tell you. Things I did. It is time you know," he whispered into her hair.

"We have been through this. I do not care; I know who you are. Whatever went on before does not matter."

"It does. It does. You need to know who you are paired with. You need to know the terrible things I am capable of. What I *was* capable of—"

"Please, let this go; whatever was done is done.

Nothing good can come of this, Adoeete," and she turned to face him.

Khon'Tor sat up and ran his hand through the silver crest in his hair. "I have seen things, witnessed events I would never have believed possible. Events that have made me understand that what is in the past is not over. Not if there are still injustices to be made right. I must do this. Even knowing that I may have to pay a terrible price, I must try to right the wrongs I committed."

Tehya sat up and leaned against him, wrapping her arms around him as far as she could. She rested her head against him.

"You have a right to know what kind of monster I am."

They remained like that for some time, each lost in their own thoughts. Each in their way concerned about what was to come. But Khon'Tor knew that what had to be, had to be.

Eventually, after Arismae had been returned, cared for, and quietened down, they slept.

Khon'Tor woke before Tehya and watched her beside him, her hair splayed out over the sleeping mat as he had seen so many times before.

Knowing what he intended to do the next day, he was aware, as he had been when first they were paired, that this might be their last night together. He selfishly kissed her lips, stirring her from her sleep. He pulled her warm form closer to him and positioned himself over her. He kissed her again gently, waking her enough to realize his intention. Slowly and with great focus, he caressed her face and told her how much he loved her. How much she had changed his life and turned everything around for him. He made love to her sweetly, taking his time, trying to create a memory that would last them both a lifetime.

The next morning, the common eating area of the cave system of Amara was filled with activity. The joyful news of the day before had created an atmosphere of giddy excitement. Khon'Tor and Tehya approached the table where Acaraho, Adia, Urilla Wuti, and the High Council members were sitting.

Oddly absent was Kurak'Kahn, the Overseer.

As Khon'Tor approached Acaraho, the High Protector turned and raised his hand to clasp that of the Leader. The exchange was not missed by Adia or the others, making them realize that the depth of what the two had experienced together had forged a very deep bond.

Once settled at the table, Khon'Tor took a moment to enjoy watching his mate eating.

"Tehya's parents were so pleased to see her. And Arismae," said Adia to Khon'Tor.

"They were," Tehya chipped in. "And they adore Arismae. I am not sure I am ever going to get her back, though. They cannot get enough of her. And I cannot wait for them to meet you, Adoeete."

Khon'Tor ran his hand through his silver crown, and suddenly, a sense of order washed over him.

Of course. We are here at Far High Hills. This was her first home. He was humbled by a feeling that without his awareness, he had been guided by some higher power. *Her parents are here. Her past is here. And so, then, is her future.*

"Where is the Overseer?" he asked.

"We have seen little of him since coming here. He has kept to himself. He is showing the wear of this. Perhaps he needed time alone," said Awan.

Under the table, Adia took Acaraho's hand, so deeply grateful at the miracle of his safe return to her. He squeezed her fingers.

"When will you tell us what happened? We are overcome with wanting to know," said Tehya.

"I believe that is best handled by Harak'Sar. The events we witnessed affect all the People, and it will take more than one of us to tell it. I believe it is best shared with as many of our people at once, and when I see Harak'Sar next, I will speak to him about an assembly," answered Khon'Tor.

"When will we be able to return to Kthama? Soon?" asked Adia. She did not want her offspring born here; she wanted to be home in familiar surroundings.

"I know you are anxious to return," said Khon'-

Tor. "But there are matters to settle here before we leave. We can discuss it after the assembly."

As he finished speaking, Urilla Wuti motioned to Harak'Sar, who had just entered. Spotting the seated Leaders, he approached their table.

"The tunnels of the Mother Stream are still clear. I sent some watchers as close as possible to Kthama while allowing for their return this morning. There is no evidence of anything unusual," he said.

"We do not believe there will be any trouble. But we do need to share what happened—the sooner, the better—and preferably with everyone at once," said Khon'Tor. "And then with all the other communities as well."

"The People already know enough of the situation for now. I suggest we wait until the males return from Kthama so they can also bear witness to exactly what happened. Then we can call the assembly. This is not Kthama, and we do not have a Great Chamber as you do. But we will arrange something outside, weather permitting, where everyone can attend at once. Commander, if you would like to meet with my High Protector, Thorak, you can make the arrangements together.

"The sooner, the better," repeated Khon'Tor. "Make the arrangements; I am ready." *I am ready. After the assembly, I will ask to meet with the High Council alone. No matter what happens, it is time. Hakani was wrong; I am not blameless for what I did. And even though the person I was, that version of me, no longer exists, no doubt the pain and suffering of what he did—of what I did—remains. And for that, there must be restitution.*

"When will you be returning to Kthama?" asked Harak'Sar, breaking into Khon'Tor's reverie.

"I realize that Amara is bursting at the seams with the addition of our people. Your resources must be strained. I suggest we return in segments, starting the day after the assembly," replied Acaraho. He rose to leave, "I have a full day ahead, so I will catch you later," and he gently brushed Adia's cheek. "If you will tell me where to find Commander Thorak, we can begin making the arrangements."

Harak'Sar beckoned, and two of his guards came over. "This is my First Guard, Dreth. Take Acaraho, High Protector of the High Rocks to Commander Thorak."

Acaraho left with the First Guard, and the conversation continued.

"Where is Kurak'Kahn?"

"We have not seen him, Harak'Sar. He continues to keep to himself," answered Lesharo'Mok.

"The members of the High Council who are here must convene before the assembly,"

"It will be a relatively small group. Without all the Leaders, there are only a few of us."

"It cannot be helped." Harak'Sar turned to the second guard.

"Go to the Overseer's quarters and ask him to come here at once."

Kurak'Kahn was in his assigned quarters, where he had spent the majority of the past few weeks alone. He needed time on his own. Lots of time on his own. The mantle of leadership was weighing heavily on his shoulders, and he grievously missed his mate, Larara.

I have no one to turn to or to council me. I need Larara. I should have sent for her long ago. But I did not want to involve her in this mess with everything else going on. But it was necessary. I hope she arrives soon.

Too many changes. Too much up in the air. I need some continuity, something to hang onto, something that is known. I need the solid foundation of Larara's love.

The clack at the door startled him. *So far, they have left me in peace. Apparently, that luxury has now run its course.* "Yes?"

"Overseer, Harak'Sar requests your presence in the eating area. I am here to escort you."

"Very well."

Once assembled, Harak'Sar moved them to a more private space.

The Leader of the Far High Hills opened the meeting, which consisted of himself, Urilla Wuti—his Healer—Kurak'Kahn, Lesharo'Mok of the Deep Valley, Khon'Tor, Adia, and Nadiwani. Risik'Tar of the Great Pines and his Healer, Tapia, were also there. Harak'Sar's mate and Tehya, both Third Rank, were also present. Missing was Harak'Sar's High

Protector, Thorak, and Acaraho, who were off planning the assembly. Guards stood outside the room, as was protocol.

"I will be brief. Khon'Tor has advised that everyone should hear together what has taken place. I agree this is the best approach. No doubt, there will be murmurs and speculation after the meeting, but at least everyone will have heard the same story at the same time. I am calling a general assembly for everyone, to be held once our males return. At this moment, my High Protector, Thorak, and High Protector Acaraho of the High Rocks are making the arrangements. Of course, the watchers outside Amara will have to be caught up later."

"Khon'Tor, do you wish to say anything now?"

Khon'Tor stood.

"The past two years have rocked the very foundation of what we believed about our past. I know that the new information has not left the High Council membership. However, I believe the time for confidentiality must end. The High Council must be prepared to make immediate plans to address the challenge facing us as a People, and to make the options public."

"Options? What options; please remind me." Kurak'Kahn was speaking out of turn.

"Overseer," said Khon'Tor', "I refer to the options we discussed when you first brought the problem of our bloodlines to our attention. At present, we have two. Cross blood with the Sarnonn or find a way to introduce the Waschini blood into ours. I am not aware that those options have changed."

"Yes, of course. I thought perhaps there was another you were withholding."

Khon'Tor frowned at the Overseer's reaction. "I am not withholding anything. I am standing here advocating for disclosure to the general population of what we have learned. The time for secrets is over." Even as he said them, his own words pierced his soul.

"That seems ironic, Khon'Tor, coming from *you*."

The High Council members exchanged glances. Adia shifted in her seat, wanting to speak up but sensing that this was not the time.

Khon'Tor stepped toward Kurak'Kahn. "Speak your mind, Overseer," he said, throwing down the challenge.

"Do you want that, Khon'Tor? Think carefully before you speak again."

Khon'Tor turned away from Kurak'Kahn to address everyone. He looked at Tehya before he began. She was sitting on the edge of her seat, worry creasing her brow. Her eyes appeared to be pleading with him, and she shook her head the slightest bit—no.

"Very well," said Khon'Tor, and he turned back to face the Overseer. "Let us have it out then."

The Overseer spoke, never taking his eyes off Khon'Tor's, "Clear the room except for the Leaders.

Adia, Urilla Wuti, and Tehya will stay. Also, send the guards away."

With that, the others left, exchanging bewildered glances as they filed out.

Once they were alone, Adia stood and announced, "I request a recess until High Protector Acaraho can join us."

"Request denied. I would not be surprised if both you and Acaraho are already well aware of what the Leader of the High Rocks is about to tell us," he said, still never moving his eyes from Khon'Tor.

Khon'Tor took the offensive, "What I believe the Overseer is alluding to, are crimes of which I am guilty, which have not themselves been fully disclosed."

The room fell silent.

Khon'Tor walked over toward Tehya and looked down at her as he spoke.

"I meant what I said. The time for secrets is over. I am prepared to make full disclosure of all of my crimes, for which I am also prepared to accept punishment."

Tehya slowly shook her head again, her eyes clearly begging him to stop. Then, in desperation, she spoke, "Khon'Tor, no. Do not do this. There is no need."

Khon'Tor softened his eyes, "There is a need, Saraste'. There is a great need for the truth finally to be told."

He pulled his eyes from Tehya and walked over to

stand in front of the Overseer, feeling his full height and the intimidating effect it was having on the shorter male. *Why now? Why are you doing this, Kurak'Kahn? And how could you possibly know anything about it? Has one of those I wronged come forward after all these years?*

Adia felt the room shifting around her, the pull of E'ranale. "Oh, by the Great Mother. Not now, not now," she said under her breath.

Urilla Wuti put her arm around Adia's shoulder, focusing her energy on settling Adia back into the present.

The Overseer took a seat at the front table.

Khon'Tor began. "More than twenty years ago, was it? I have lost track. No matter. Decades ago, I stood before you all as the Healer, Adia, accused me of attacking her, and impregnating her with my seed. You all remember the events that followed. You, the High Council, asked why I should not be banished. Adia took the floor and admonished you for your harsh judgment and withdrew her accusation. At that point, your hands were tied, and there was nothing you could do to punish me for my crime.

Khon'Tor looked at Tehya. Her eyes were wide, and he could see her hands were shaking. *This is it, and I should already have told her; it is no way for her to find out. But, since I have lost her, nothing matters now except justice for those I wronged.* "No doubt you have carried animosity toward me since then, and rightfully so. Some will tell you I have changed—and I have—but that does not expunge the crimes I committed against Adia."

"But it was not just her, was it?" The Overseer's eyes narrowed with hatred as he addressed Khon'-Tor, and everyone shifted in their seats.

Adia clutched Urilla Wuti's hand—hard—and held on for dear life.

"My attack on the Healer, Adia, was precipitated by a long period of extreme stress—"

Just then, Acaraho entered. Seeing the bewildered faces and feeling the tension in the air, he elected to stand against the wall as was customary in his role as High Protector.

"—but my attack on Adia was not the only one. There were others. Other maidens I took Without Their Consent."

The High Council Overseer rose to his feet, arms stiff and face contorted.

"Others. How many others?" demanded Kurak'Kahn.

"Three."

No one moved.

"Where are they? *Who are they*?" demanded the Overseer, slamming his fist down on the table.

"I will not disclose their identities to you," Khon'Tor replied calmly.

"*You* are not in a position to withhold anything!" Kurak'Kahn came out from around the table and stormed toward Khon'Tor. "As of this moment, you are stripped of the leadership of the High Rocks."

Khon'Tor had expected that and steeled himself further. From the corner of his eye, he saw Adia get up and sit next to Tehya. He could not bring himself to look at his mate.

"I will not disclose their identities to you for their protection. I will, however, disclose them to someone you appoint so that each may be asked if she wishes my crime against her to be made public."

"*Krellshar!*" shouted the Overseer. "Just another attempt to hide your wrongdoing."

Urilla Wuti stood. "No, Overseer. Khon'Tor is right. Revealing who they are would be a further violation. Since none of them has come forward, we must assume they do not wish it to be known."

The Overseer snorted. "Since the victims are females, I turn this inquisition over to you. You are to contact them and determine their state of mind in this matter. You are right, though it seems impossible; some of them may wish to let Khon'Tor's crimes against them die in the past."

Khon'Tor found the resolve to look over at Tehya. Knowing he did not deserve forgiveness, he wished to search her eyes for it anyway. But she sat frozen, head down, eyes averted.

"Overseer. I ask for Bak'tah-Awhidi," said Khon'Tor.

"No!" Tehya jerked her head up and rose to her feet.

"No, no!" She almost staggered to stand before the Overseer.

"On what grounds, Khon'Tor? Your mate has committed no crime. It is you who is at fault."

"That is exactly the basis on which I request our pairing be set aside. Tehya is innocent. Our daughter is innocent. Their association with me must be severed so their lives can go on untainted by my crimes."

Tehya screamed at the Overseer. "I deny Bak'tah-Awhidi!"

She spun to look at Khon'Tor, "You have no right to do this," she shouted, her body tense with fury.

"You are wrong, Tehya," declared Kurak'Kahn. "He does have the right. But since you have refused it, which is your right as the fault is not yours, his request for Bak'tah-Awhidi is denied."

Tehya sagged, and stepping forward, Acaraho helped her back to her seat.

"Then remove her from the rest of the proceedings," Khon'Tor demanded.

"Also denied. Your days of demanding anything are over, Khon'Tor," said Kurak'Kahn. "She is Third Rank, and the matter at hand directly affects her community since you are their Leader. She has a right to be here."

"It is not fair that she be subjected to this." Khon'Tor had raised his voice, and he stepped toward Kurak'Kahn.

"No, it is quite the opposite. It is very fair. Tehya needs to know exactly what type of monster she is paired with—especially since she has refused for your union to be set aside," snarled Kurak'Kahn.

The Overseer then addressed Tehya. "If you wish to ask for Bak'tah-Awhidi after this is over, I will grant it for cause."

Lesharo'Mok of the Deep Valley stood to address the others. "I suggest we take a recess. Emotions are flared. Tempers are raised. This information is difficult for everyone to assimilate. Kurak'Kahn has named Urilla Wuti as the director of this investigation, but others should be involved as well. I propose High Protector Acaraho and First Guard Awan—once he arrives with our returning males, both of the People of the High Rocks."

"They are from Khon'Tor's community. There will be bias," the Overseer objected.

"I know them both well; their reputations are renowned. There will be no bias." Lesharo'Mok glared at Kurak'Kahn. Adia had never seen her uncle so inflamed.

"The crimes Khon'Tor has committed are private in nature," Lesharo'Mok continued, "as the Healer has pointed out. Allowing this information out of the room will only harm them further. It must be contained as much as possible. Acaraho is already involved."

Harak'Sar stood. "I agree."

"Very well," Kurak'Kahn agreed grudgingly.

"I request that the Healer, Adia, join the group," said Urilla Wuti.

"On what grounds?"

"On the grounds, Overseer, that she was a victim of the same atrocity that Khon'Tor has just said he committed against others. And she is a Healer. Her presence will be crucial to helping them through this process. The fact that two males have been proposed and you do not see a problem with that shows *your* bias. And your ignorance."

Kurak'Kahn's upper lip curled, the start of a snarl, but he said nothing. After a moment, he waved his hand in agreement.

"I further propose that the victims be allowed to determine Khon'Tor's punishment. They should be the ones to pass judgment; no male can understand the damage that has been done," added Urilla Wuti.

Khon'Tor did not object. "I am prepared to accept whatever punishment they decide."

"Even execution?" challenged Kurak'Kahn.

"Yes."

Tehya bent over and curled her arms around her head as if to shut everything out and started slowly rocking back and forth in her seat.

Seeing the state she was in, Khon'Tor nodded toward her, "Please, Overseer."

"Alright. This meeting is adjourned. Put this out of your minds during the assembly. We will focus on the topic later. Anyone who discusses this matter with anyone not already named or involved will permanently be removed from the High Council—in disgrace. You are all dismissed."

The moment the meeting ended, Tehya jumped up and ran to Khon'Tor. She flew into his arms, and he caught her up gently. The others left to give them some privacy.

"No, no, no, what have you done? They can order you killed. Why, Adoeete? Why?"

"Tehya, I do not know by what miracle you do not hate me. You have every right. How is it you are still standing by me? You should have let them grant Bak'tah-Awhidi. No matter the outcome, this is no life for you, tied to me."

He pulled her away from him to look at her. "How, how can you forgive me for what I have done?"

Through her tears, she told him, "After we were first paired and Haan and Hakani had arrived, Hakani trapped me in one of the tunnels and told me that you enjoyed taking females Without Their Consent. At the time, I did not believe her. Later, when Akar'Tor held me captive, he told me the same thing but also that you had attacked Adia. I did not believe him, either, but I knew I had to consider it as a possibility. I could not reconcile what they told me you had done, with whom I knew you to be. But over time, I came to realize that if what they said was true, you were no longer the monster who committed these crimes—that the you who did those things no longer existed. So many at Kthama said how much you had changed. People can change. And they deserve forgiveness when a transformation is genuine."

"I do not deserve you. Or your forgiveness. But I do not have the forgiveness of the others I wronged, and I must do it for them."

"I could lose you forever."

"There are worse things, Tehya. Better I lose my life than lose my soul. Better to risk this life, than risk spending eternity without you."

"Are you saying you believe there truly is a krell?" she asked.

"In the past, I dismissed it as a story meant to frighten offspring into behaving. Now, after what I have seen, I consider it a real possibility," Khon'Tor answered.

In the hallway, Urilla Wuti, Adia, and Acaraho stood talking.

"We must learn who these females are and make arrangements to speak with them discreetly," said Adia.

"It seems the Overseer almost expected this. It looked as if he was goading Khon'Tor into something. Did he perhaps know of these other assaults?" wondered Urilla Wuti.

"He knows something. I am sure we will find out soon enough. But Khon'Tor was prepared to confess anyway; I sensed that clearly," said Adia. Then she continued, "I am worried about Tehya. She has gained some weight, but she is still too thin, and this will make everything worse. Perhaps we should insist she start taking something for the strain."

Acaraho was watching his mate closely. He knew her well enough to be aware that Khon'Tor's confession had rocked her. She had believed that what he did to her was an isolated instance, the result of a state of uncontrolled rage inflamed in him by Hakani. Which might, in part, be correct, but which did not explain the other violations. And in some part of her, she would be blaming herself for hiding his crime, even though it was a decision made to protect the community from civil war.

"I am retiring for a while. What about you?" asked Urilla.

"I need some time alone," said Adia.

"I do not think you should be alone right now," said her mate.

She shook her head. "I will be alright. Please—"

With difficulty, Acaraho conceded. "I will be with Thorak, checking on the general assembly plans. I will meet up with you there," he said, before leaving.

Adia returned to the quarters that had been assigned to her. She went over to the sleeping mat and curled up into a ball.

What have I done? I was so sure I did the right thing by not turning in Khon'Tor. The other females—those Khon'Tor attacked—their suffering is also on my head.

How do I live with it? I was called to be a Healer, and yet what I did has caused immeasurable pain and suffering.

"Father, oh, how I need to speak with you again. I need you to hold me. I feel I have lost my way. I am about to bring Acaraho's son into the world, but what kind of world am I bringing him into? Everything that made our lives safe, predictable, comforting—every foundation is being rocked. I was so sure I did the right thing by not accusing or punishing Khon'-Tor. But now, decades later, we are at the same point. If what he did is disclosed, our community will come apart. They have already been through so much—the revelation that the Sarnonn exist, the existence of Kthama Minor, the attack of the rebel Sarnonn. Even if Khon'Tor's crimes do not come out, he is no longer the Leader; the Overseer has stripped him of his position. How will that be explained? And there is no heir to take his place—none that he can claim."

She curled over to her other side and let the tears come.

From the Corridor, Adia's father, Apenimon, and E'ranale witnessed Adia's hour of distress.

"Can we not just bring her here? She needs to feel my arms around her," he pleaded.

"She feels my call and has refused it. You know full well it is best for her that unless there is an imminent threat of failure, she must find her way through this without our direct intervention. She is a fighter; she will survive."

"She will survive, yes. But at what cost, E'ranale? If the cost is her sense of safety, her happiness, her faith in the Great Spirit, and her budding belief in the Order of Functions, what will there be left for her?"

"Even if that is the price, what will be left for her will have to be enough. She has her calling as Healer, the love of her mate, Acaraho, and her responsibility for her soon-to-be-born son. We must not forget that."

Apenimon sighed. "I thought that when I left the realm of Etera, all this anguish and worry would cease."

"You sound like your daughter, who questioned why Lifrin could feel anguish here over the little brother she left behind. If that were true, what would be the point of continued existence? It is our love for each other that makes consciousness worth the price it brings. Connection carries vulnerability. There is no way for it to be otherwise." E'ranale sighed. "I have been calling her, but she does not yield. We must wait. That is what we have to do."

CHAPTER 5

A few days passed. The beauty of spring was beginning to blossom around Amara. There was enough cloud cover to make the spring afternoon pleasantly cool as the People of the Far High Hills, and their visitors from the High Rocks gathered outside, waiting for the assembly to begin.

The onlookers fidgeted and chatted among themselves, eyes darting nervously around the group. Rumors abounded about the purpose of the meeting.

The High Council members were also in the audience as Harak'Sar took his place at the top of an embankment that overlooked the crowd. Awan and the other males had arrived and some stood behind him with the Leaders of the High Rocks.

Harak'Sar stepped forward, his signal that he was about to speak. The crowd immediately fell silent.

"As you are aware from our meeting some time

ago, the Sarnonn do exist. As you are also aware, there was a serious risk of an attack on Kthama from a rebel Sarnonn faction. That is why the elderly, unpaired males, females, and offspring were evacuated from Kthama. Some of them are sheltered here, and others at the Deep Valley." He motioned to those standing behind him. "It was due to remarkable events that Kthama did not fall to the Sarnonn. With me are members of the High Rocks who witnessed these events of monumental importance, and of which we need to make you aware. I will now turn the assembly over to them to share with you what they witnessed."

Only the sounds of birdsong broke the silence. A lone crow watched from high in a nearby oak.

Khon'Tor took the stage. With the Rah-hora dissolved, there was much to cover, including what the People had not yet heard about the Age of Darkness, the existence of the Mothoc, and the split of the Mothoc into the Sarnonn and the People. He spoke for quite a while, but, barely noticing the passage of time, the crowd remained captivated, all eyes fixed on him. Finally, he got to the approach of the rebel Sarnonn toward Kthama, their belief that all was lost and that Haan's people had betrayed them, and then the final intervention of Haan's group. When he described the manifestation of Straf'Tor, members of the crowd gasped and exchanged glances.

When he finally finished, the Healers came to the front to explain further.

A few hours had passed by the time all had spoken. But now everyone present knew about the unbelievable events of the past few days and the specter of extinction that hung over their heads.

Harak'Sar took over to end the meeting.

"I realize that what you have just heard is difficult to take in. Perhaps it seems unbelievable, but the witnesses speak to the truth of what you have been told. As we move forward, we must find a way to address the pressing issue of our bloodlines, and you will hear more about this later. We have every reason to believe that we can find a solution—we have options. Over the next few days, the People of the High Rocks will return to Kthama, and routine will return. But, knowing what we now know, things will never be the same again." He paused. "I know you are all tired, so we will adjourn for now."

As long as the meeting had taken, it took nearly an equal amount of time for the assembly to disperse. People stood around discussing the events that had just been described, and the uncertain future that lay before them.

Harak'Sar turned to those who had spoken during the assembly. "No doubt you will be approached about what you have shared. Answer as best you can; everyone needs to realize that this is the truth, as impossible as it sounds."

Kurak'Kahn addressed them too. "It is also appropriate that you travel to the Deep Valley with Lesharo'Mok and share what you have shared here. I suggest that the appropriate parties leave almost immediately as we have further business to attend to upon the Leaders' return here."

"Now, Urilla Wuti, Adia, and Acaraho, please stay for a moment," said Overseer Kurak'Kahn.

Once alone with the two Healers and Acaraho, he continued, "As soon as this information is shared with the Deep Valley, I expect you quickly to identify the other females Khon'Tor assaulted. And I expect to be promptly informed of any events which transpire related to this investigation. I also expect Khon'-Tor's mate to be present at all punishments exacted. Including execution, if it comes to that."

After he was finished, the three silently left.

Acaraho, Urilla Wuti, Adia, and Khon'Tor met privately that afternoon, and Khon'Tor gave them the names of those he had assaulted. Tar'sa of the Deep Valley and Kayah, who was mated to Akule. The third, the young female he had attacked outside Kthama at the Ashwea Awhidi, he could not identify. He knew neither her name nor where she came from. It was a dead end.

"Kayah," said Adia. "Kayah is Akule's mate. He is here with the males who came from Kthama. As soon as the others return from the Deep Valley, I suggest we start with her, as she is here with the other High Rocks females," she continued, trying to hold her feelings at bay.

Khon'Tor and the witnesses of the events that had taken place at High Rocks, along with Lesharo'Mok, Leader of the Deep Valley, journeyed there and shared the same story they had just told everyone at the Far High Hills.

❂

After several days, Khon'Tor and those witnesses who were not originally from the Deep Valley returned, as did Lesharo'Mok, who was needed back at the Far High Hills to continue the High Council investigation into Khon'Tor's crimes.

Now that it was time, Adia went to find Kayah to take her to the meeting room where she and Urilla Wuti would be speaking with her in private.

❂

"What is this about? Why am I meeting with two Healers? Am I ill and do not know it?"

"No, Kayah. As far as we know, you are perfectly healthy. But a crime has been brought to light. A crime committed against you a few years ago, before you came to the High Rocks to be paired with Akule. Do you know what I am referring to?" asked Adia.

Kayah's countenance crumbled, and she squeezed her eyes shut.

"I have kept my silence all this time. Yes, of course I know what you are speaking of. Khon'Tor, the renowned and respected, great *Leader* of the High Rocks, who took me Without My Consent while I was still a maiden. It was during his visit here, just before the Ashwea Awhidi."

Adia paused before continuing. "And you never came forward? Does your mate, Akule, know about it?"

"No, Akule does not. For months after it happened, I could barely function. At first, I was terrified I had been seeded, though, by the time of the Ashwea Awhidi, I knew I was not. I did my best to put it out of my mind and make a life for myself—despite having to live at the High Rocks with my attacker as my Leader."

"Khon'Tor has confessed to taking you Without Your Consent," said Urilla Wuti. "The High Council has decided that it will be up to you to determine his punishment."

Kayah looked up, and her tone became harsh. "What he did ruined my life. I have never gotten over it. It has been hard on my pairing with Akule. I wanted to enjoy being paired, and I know he waited a long time. I have done my best, but I am not the mate he deserves—all of because of what Khon'Tor did to me.

"You are wondering why I did not come forward. Why I did not tell anyone what Khon'Tor did. You cannot understand why I kept silent. But who would believe me? He was Khon'Tor, the *great Leader of the People*. No one would have believed that he would risk his position over a mere female. He could have anyone he wanted; why would he have to take one by force? So I kept quiet. I did not want my life to be publicly ruined by accusing a legend of such an atrocity."

Adia forced her mouth shut. She wanted to assure Kayah that she did indeed understand. But she could not—not without also disclosing Khon'-Tor's crime against her.

Then, after a moment, Kayah asked, "What are my options for punishment?" Her eyes were hard and icy.

"The standard means of punishment is whipping. But Khon'Tor has declared that he will accept whatever you decide is just."

Kayah fell into silence.

"Do I get to watch?" she asked.

Adia barely suppressed a frown and a grimace in time.

"If that will help you heal, yes," answered Urilla Wuti.

"Fifty lashes."

Urilla Wuti closed her eyes. It was excessive. "Kayah," she said softly, "*fifty lashes—*"

"You are right; it should be far more for what I have suffered all these years!"

Though none of the females had ever seen anyone whipped before, there had been very occasional stories of it from other communities. There were few punishments, whipping being the standard and banishment being the most severe. Either Kayah had missed the point of Urilla Wuti's comment, or her bloodlust was overpowering any sense of proportion.

"I will make arrangements. It will be done as soon as possible. Do you wish Akule to be present?" interrupted Adia.

"No. I do not want my mate ever to learn of this. There would be no benefit. And after this is over, we will please not speak of it again."

By the next day, the secluded area where Khon'Tor's punishment would be exacted had been prepared, a tiny alcove outside, in among some high rock walls. The appointed members, those ordered present by the Overseer, were seated on wood stumps and boulders—Harak'Sar, Risik'Tar, Lesharo'Mok, the two Healers, Nadiwani, and Tehya. Acaraho stood off to the side.

Acaraho had told Khon'Tor ahead of time that he was not to be executed but that the punishment would be severe and to prepare himself. He felt he owed the ex-Leader that much.

Khon'Tor was brought in and told to face everyone while he heard the details of the punishment decided on by Kayah. He tried to keep his eyes straight ahead, knowing she was there. He did not want to traumatize her further.

Kurak'Kahn paced as he spoke, unable to disguise his pleasure in the moment, his hand clasped around the handle of a whip. "Khon'Tor, you have confessed to the crime of taking Kayah of the High Rocks Without Her Consent. She has confirmed that the crime took place and has decided your punishment will be fifty lashes, which shall be administered to you here and now."

At hearing the number, Tehya slumped forward, covering her eyes. It was only then that Kayah noticed her. Kayah had not realized that his mate would be present, and the color drained from her face.

"Overseer," Kayah interrupted. "Should his mate not be removed? She does not need to see this."

"She will be removed if she requests it. Otherwise, no."

Khon'Tor turned and faced one of the rock walls, extending his arms overhead, palms out to brace himself. He steepled his legs for balance and tightened his core.

The Overseer stepped forward, drew back the lash in his hand, and let loose with all his might.

The leather snapped and cut deeply through Khon'Tor's skin, sending streams of blood coursing down his back and splattering everywhere. Khon'Tor winced involuntarily.

Another. And Another. With each stroke, the sickening sound of hide cutting living flesh echoed around the space. After fifteen lashes, there was no place to strike other than on top of the existing deep, bloody wounds.

Acaraho could tell Khon'Tor was in excruciating pain. Blood was pooling on the ground around his feet. The smell of it tainted the air. Acaraho stepped forward, "Overseer—"

"Get out of the way, Commander," ordered Kurak'Kahn.

Acaraho did not move.

"*I told you to move, High Protector.*" This time there was steel in his voice. His hand clenched the handle of the whip almost as if he was considering using it against Acaraho.

Tehya burst from her seat and ran forward. "No, no, please. Can you not see you are killing him?"

"Step back, Tehya," said the Overseer, but she ducked between him and Khon'Tor.

"This is not justice; it is brutality," she shouted. "He cannot take any more." Then she looked at Kayah, "Please, Kayah. It is too much."

Khon'Tor, using all his strength to remain standing, painfully turned his head to address his mate.

"Tehya. Hush, Saraste'," his voice was hoarse with pain. "Overseer, please, remove her."

Giving no quarter, Kurak'Kahn replied, "She has not asked to be removed. Step aside, Acaraho. Step aside, Tehya."

"No. I will not step aside. *You are killing Khon'Tor,*" shouted Tehya.

At that moment, Adia rose and came and placed

her hands on Tehya's shoulders. "The punishment was not death, Overseer," she hissed. "It is enough; he cannot take any more."

"The punishment has not been delivered. The victim has ordered fifty lashes. We are at fifteen. There are thirty-five to go." Kurak'Kahn would not give any ground.

Urilla Wuti stood up abruptly. "Enough, Overseer!" she shouted. "It is obvious he will not survive thirty-five more lashes. The victim did not order him killed; she ordered fifty lashes in ignorance of what that entails. It is not a means by which you can enact your own vengeance."

Kurak'Kahn clamped his eyes on her. "*How dare you,*" he snapped.

"I do not know what has caused this, Overseer," Urilla Wuti continued, her voice raised, "But it is obvious you have a personal vendetta against Khon'-Tor. We all see it. You need to recuse yourself from this proceeding and this punishment."

"You are all in contempt," bellowed Kurak'Kahn. He turned back to Khon'Tor and drew back the lash, ready to let it fly. Before he could complete the stroke, Acaraho was on him.

The struggle was over immediately. Kurak'Kahn was no match for Acaraho, who had easily ripped the whip from the Overseer's hand and thrown it out of reach across the alcove. He quickly brought the Overseer's hands around behind his back and pinned him up against the bloody rock wall, his body trapping him in place.

Kayah caught Tehya's gaze and finally rose to her feet.

"Stop. Stop it, everyone. The Healer is right. It is enough. He cannot survive any more. I declare Kah-Sol 'Rin. *Justice has been served.*"

Tehya ran to Khon'Tor and embraced him, ignoring the blood that was now being smeared all over her coverings. He winced in pain as her arms almost encircled his waist.

Nadiwani ran out of the area to one of the guards stationed a way back and asked him to find First Guard Awan of the High Rocks and bring him immediately.

Khon'Tor had slid down the bloodied wall to his knees, taking Tehya with him. He was bleeding profusely, his back a plain of raw, mutilated meat.

First Guard Awan returned within minutes, with Akule following behind. Everyone stood horrified as they recognized Kayah's mate.

"Take the Overseer to his quarters and keep him confined," commanded Acaraho.

They looked at the High Protector as if he were crazy.

"On my orders. *Now*," Acaraho barked.

Akule could not help himself. "What is going on here," he asked, his eyes landing on his mate near the front of the group.

"Now, Akule. Do it now," repeated Acaraho. He wanted to get Akule out of there immediately.

Akule scowled at Kayah, then spun around, and with one of the guards, removed Kurak'Kahn as ordered.

"This is not over. It is not over!" the Overseer shouted as they hustled him out of sight.

"Awan, help me with Khon'Tor," said Acaraho. "We need to get him to his quarters as quickly as possible." To the remaining guard, he barked, "You, go on ahead and clear the way. We need privacy."

Kayah was pale as a ghost. *Akule. What was Akule doing here? He is not even a guard; he is a watcher. He has always been a watcher. He must somehow have come with Awan.*

Seeing them carry out the weak and bloodied Khon'Tor kicked Adia into Healer mode.

They gingerly laid Khon'Tor face-down on the sleeping mat in the quarters assigned to him and Tehya. Nadiwani began tending to him, trying her best not to hurt him further. Adia heated water to make willow bark tea to help ease the pain, though it would not cut it by much.

"Is he going to live?" asked Tehya.

"I do not know. The wounds are severe and there is always a risk of infection. If Khon'Tor does live, he will carry the scars on his back forever, and they will be considerable." Adia explained. Then she continued, "If you still want to stay with him, Tehya, now would be the time to tell him. If not, then I under-stand, and I ask you to keep your silence."

Tears rolled down Tehya's cheeks, and she went to Khon'Tor's side, crouching down next to him and speaking as close into his ear as possible.

"Adoeete," she brushed the matted hair back from the side of his head. "You must listen to me; I am giving the orders now. You must fight to live. You must not leave me here alone. I love you. I need you. *I am not prepared to consider living without you.* I do not care what you did. I do not care about any of it; my love for you has not changed and never will. Please stay with me; Arismae and I need you desper-ately. Please, my love. Please do not leave us."

In as much pain as he was, Khon'Tor reached out his hand to Tehya. She grasped it and held it as tightly as she could.

That night, the fever hit him. Hard.

As soon as he could, Acaraho went to find Harak'Sar. In having the Overseer removed by force and confined to his quarters, the High Protector had stepped way out of line.

"A moment, please," he interrupted the Leader, who was talking with two guards.

They moved away, and Acaraho spoke. "Adik'Tar, I apologize. I overstepped my authority."

"You did right. I told my guards to obey your

orders as they would Thorak's. Let us go to the Overseer now."

When they arrived, the guards opened the door, and Harak'Sar and Acaraho entered.

Kurak'Kahn jumped up to face them as they came in. "Release me at once."

"Not just yet, Overseer. You ordered the lashings to continue knowing full well they would result in Khon'Tor's death. Yet the victim had not ordered him executed."

"His death would have been an unfortunate consequence of administering the full penalty. It is not over. He must still endure the balance when he recovers."

"The other High Council members will not agree."

"I am the Overseer. It does not matter if none of you agree."

Harak'Sar glanced at Acaraho and back. "Kurak'Kahn, what is behind this vindictiveness? I realize that Khon'Tor's crimes are indefensible, but when did you begin to hate him so?"

The Overseer looked up and glared at Harak'Sar. "You think I hate Khon'Tor? Well, what if I do? And why should I not? Has he not done enough? I am sick of the drama and problems coming out of the High Rocks. I am fed up with all of you," he spat, glaring at Acaraho.

The two left Kurak'Kahn, and on the way out, Harak'Sar gave orders for the guards to be doubled.

The Leader turned to Acaraho. "I have heard enough. I am going to recommend to the others that Kurak'Kahn be removed as Overseer. It has never happened before, but these are extenuating circumstances. We must adapt if we are to survive. He is no longer able to serve objectively in that capacity, nor, I would say, on the High Council at all."

"I agree. I will come with you."

On the way to find Risik'Tar and Lesharo'Mok, Acaraho stopped to check on Khon'Tor.

"What is his condition?" he asked Adia.

"Tenuous. We do not know if he will survive."

At hearing this, Acaraho told the other Leaders he would catch up shortly.

Once they were gone, Adia said, "Acaraho, there is something you must know about Khon'Tor's wounds—"

Harak'Sar, Risik'Tar, and Lesharo'Mok continued their meeting without Acaraho.

"Whether Khon'Tor recovers or not, the High Rocks is without a Leader," said Harak'Sar. "The Overseer stripped him of his leadership while he still had the authority to do so, and I have to agree with that decision."

"For now, I suggest the interim leadership fall to Acaraho," said Risik'Tar. "Responsibility for execution of orders always falls to the High Protector anyway, should the Leader be absent or incapacitated."

"It is a natural progression for the High Protector to lead until the High Council can determine a solution," said Harak'Sar. "If we agree, we will need to tell the People of the High Rocks. Except I am not sure what to say."

"We can wait, Harak'Sar. As it is, at present, we have enough on our hands to deal with," said Lesharo'Mok.

"Very true," agreed Harak'Sar. "When this storm passes, we need to reconvene the full High Council. Much has transpired of which the Leaders of the other communities are not aware," added Risik'Tar.

"Alright. Adjourned for now," said Harak'Sar.

Once Risik'Tar was out of earshot, the Leader of the Far High Hills turned to Lesharo'Mok. "We are forgetting Nootau."

Silence.

Nootau. Sired by Khon'Tor, he carried the 'Tor line and had a right to the leadership. But putting him in place would mean revealing that Khon'Tor had seeded Adia.

"Khon'Tor is the father of Nootau. He has a right to the 'Tor leadership," continued Harak'Sar.

"Listen to what you are saying. Appointing Nootau would mean revealing that Khon'Tor is his father. We do not have that right. That would have to be Adia's decision; it was her love for the People and her desire to protect them that caused her to keep silent all these years. We have no right to betray her confidence."

"Dire times call for exceptions to be made," countered Harak'Sar.

"Dire times or not, no more lives will be destroyed by this High Council, at least not with my participation," Lesharo'Mok stated firmly.

"We are just discharging our responsibilities."

"*Are we*?" Lesharo'Mok was cynical. "Even though we took a vow of objectivity, are we always able to rise above our inner conflicts? Look at what has just happened with the Overseer. If Tehya had not objected, would we have stood by and let Kurak'Kahn deliver the full number of lashes? The Overseer must have known it would kill Khon'Tor."

"Acaraho intervened."

"It was only the females' voices that stopped it. All the more reason to have them permanent council members; we need the balance that softer voices can bring."

Harak'Sar looked off into the distance, considering Lesharo'Mok's remarks.

"Let us pray that Khon'Tor survives. At least we will not have that on our conscience," Harak'Sar finally said.

"And if he does—what of the matter of the second female? What of her judgment against him?"

The two males stood silently, the mantle of leadership weighing heavily on their shoulders.

Back in their guest quarters, Kayah braced for Akule's questions. It did not take long for them to surface; the moment he came in, he began questioning her.

"What was going on, Kayah? Why was Khon'Tor bleeding? What was your role in it? Explain this to me."

Kayah had never seen Akule so upset.

"I do not wish to talk about it. It is private," and she turned away.

"*Private*? Something is going on, something serious involving my mate and my Leader? And you do not think I have a right to know?"

"I do not want you to know. Nothing good will come of it. It is something that happened a while ago."

"It may have happened a while ago, whatever it was, but it has not passed. This afternoon was proof enough of that. Your current state is proof of that. Now *tell me*."

Kayah broke down and told Akule the entire story.

When she finished, he was speechless for a while. And then the rest of it fell into place.

I share in this. This is partly my fault. I knew; I knew in my heart that Khon'Tor had found Adia and attacked her. I knew it as well as I knew anything. The timing, the fact that he ordered me, a watcher, to replace the guard at

Kthama's entrance. The fact that he questioned me about that evening, all of a sudden making conversation with me at odd times when before he barely knew my name. I was a coward, and my silence made it possible for him to continue. Had I spoken up, this would never have happened to her.

Overcome with guilt, Akule did not know what to say but knew he had to say something. He softened his voice and relaxed his posture. "I am so sorry this was done to you and that you have suffered alone all these years; I wish you had told me. I understand the cause of the difficulties between us now," he said.

She just nodded quietly, unable to stop her tears.

"So I walked in on Khon'Tor's punishment," he stated matter-of-factly.

"Yes. They said I could choose anything, even execution. That he had agreed to accept whatever I decided. I asked for fifty lashes."

Akule could not stop a sharp intake of breath. He recalled the vision of the Overseer and the bloodied whip lying on the ground. Even for a male of Khon'-Tor's health and vigor, it was a serious sentence.

"I did not know. I promise you I did not realize what it meant. After fifteen, his mate, Tehya, begged for it to stop. They took him away and I am afraid to ask if he is still alive," she said softly.

Akule took control of himself and went to sit beside her. He pulled her into him and let her release her anguish in his arms.

CHAPTER 6

Tehya had not left Khon'Tor's side for days, only stopping to nurse Arismae and tend to her care. Nadiwani and Adia had done their best to console her and get her to eat because her skin was pulled tightly over her bones, her arms even frailer than before. The little weight she had gained since coming to Far High Hills was gone. Her milk production was down, and eventually, they had to arrange for a wet nurse to help feed Arismae. Exhausted, she took to lying alongside Khon'Tor. Nadiwani, Adia, and Urilla Wuti took turns caring for them, but it seemed hopeless.

An infection had taken hold, and they could not get Khon'Tor's fever down. Unless a miracle happened, both Healers knew it was just a matter of time before they would lose them both.

Back in her quarters, Adia was not feeling well and was resting for a moment. She was still fighting the pull from E'ranale, afraid to leave Etera's realm for fear that Tehya or Khon'Tor might take an even more serious turn for the worse while she was away. Finally, almost having lost the ability to function, she told Urilla Wuti that she had to surrender. She lay down and quieted her mind, Urilla Wuti at her side. Within moments Adia was once again in E'ranale's presence.

"Why did you not come, Adia? I have been calling to you for some time."

"I am sorry, E'ranale. We are struggling with so much right now. Everything is falling apart. Khon'-Tor, Tehya; we fear we may lose them both. Is my father here? Can I see him?"

"You must learn to trust me, Adia. And I know you long to see Apenimon again. You will, in time. Your need for the comfort of your father's arms proves how strong the tie of love is. In contrast, the will to live, to stay within the realm of Etera, is sometimes tenuous in times of trial—even more so when your loved ones are no longer there. There is much that can break it. And the trials Khon'Tor and Tehya have experienced have pushed them to the brink of utter despair."

"Yes. But despite everything that has been revealed, Tehya still loves Khon'Tor. And he loves her. More than life itself. They both do."

"It is not often that a person truly changes. And if

the change is genuine, they nearly always carry deep remorse over their actions. And remorse, like regret, is difficult to live with. It taints every good experience with the poison of guilt—that happiness, pleasure, love are not things they deserve. And sometimes, if life does not serve up the punishment they secretly feel they have coming, they will find a way to bring it on themselves. The answer to what is needed of you next is right there in front of you."

By the Great Mother. Khon'Tor wants to die—and Tehya's love is taking her with him. "Thank you, E'ranale."

"You are welcome, Adia. Stay strong. This storm has almost passed."

Adia opened her eyes to see Urilla Wuti still sitting next to her, dozing.

"Wake up, Urilla Wuti. Time is of the essence. Help me back to Khon'Tor and Tehya."

Acaraho was there with Nadiwani when the Healers entered. "I was looking for you. How are things going?" he asked.

"I think I know what I must do to help them," said Adia.

The sound of talking roused Tehya from her half-sleep, and she turned enough to look up at Adia. "Please, is there nothing else you can do?" she whispered.

"There is something I can do to reach Khon'Tor, but I will need your help. It means that you and I will have to join together closer than two people ever do. You will know my experiences and my emotions, and I will know yours. It is only through this Healer's ritual that I can take you to him."

"Anything. Anything, please," Tehya begged.

"You need to understand that what he did to me, you will experience as I did. Be sure, please."

"I am willing. I am so sorry, Adia; perhaps my knowing your suffering will help ease it," she said faintly.

Nootau, Nimida, Adia thought. Perhaps Khon'Tor was right, *the time for secrets is over.*

Adia and Nadiwani gently moved Tehya over, so there was room on the mat for Adia. She carefully slipped between them, taking first Khon'Tor's hand and then Tehya's. Urilla Wuti sat at Adia's feet, where she could make contact with Adia if necessary. Though their abilities were far enough advanced that contact was not necessary, they were driven to use it in case it might help in some way. Frowning, Acaraho watched from a few feet away.

Adia closed her eyes, and Urilla Wuti did the same. Then Adia reached out toward Khon'Tor. At first, she could not find him. Part of her panicked—was he already gone beyond her reach, though his body somehow still lived? She reached deeply, then deeper still. She entered inky darkness, at once both a lonely, empty void and a smothering bleakness. It was almost more than she could bear. Her soul instinctively railed against the isolation and the heaviness, yet she pushed herself farther inward. Then, finally, in the abject darkness, she found the small flame of what used to be Khon'Tor. She surrounded him with her soul—with love, with protection—and coaxed him into a connection with her. He resisted, but she did not relent until, finally, her soul was shallowly interlaced with the washed-out echo of the soul that had burned so strong. Even joining at such a tenuous level, Adia was immediately overcome by the excruciating physical pain his body was suffering. Despite the agony, she willed herself to move closer and deeper until she and Khon'Tor were one. She used all her self-control to help him push the pain aside so he could experience her presence. Beyond that physical pain, there was a burning lake of mental anguish. Regret. Isolation. Remorse. Self-recrimination. And the self-hatred E'ranale had spoken of. It was clear that Khon'Tor wanted to die. He wanted to be punished for what he had done so he could find peace, and no punishment except death was severe enough to appease his judgment of himself. The self-loathing and thrashing anguish of his soul threatened to force her into his self-exile in the pits of krell.

Adia moaned out loud, and Urilla Wuti joined in to help strengthen Adia's connection with herself, lest his despair overcome her. Urilla Wuti encased Adia's soul with her own energy, grounding her

enough that, finally, she was strong enough to maintain her connection with Khon'Tor and yet still
extend herself. Momentarily shored up, Adia then
reached out to find Tehya.

In the background, Acaraho was becoming
agitated. Adia's unconscious moans were breaking
his self-control, and he paced back and forth.

The fingertips of Adia's consciousness touched
Tehya's. With no effort, they were laced together as
one. The deep heartache, the fear of losing Khon'Tor,
consumed them both. Adia began to sob uncon-
trollably.

"Urilla, you must stop it. It is hurting her," and
Acaraho headed toward the three prone figures.

Nadiwani grabbed Acaraho by the arm and
pulled, trying to turn him away. "Look at me. Look at
me. *This is who Adia is.* This is her calling; she chose
this, and you cannot take this from her. If you do, you
deny her the very essence of who she was meant to
be. You condemn her to be less than was given her."

Acaraho closed his eyes and fought as hard as he
could to maintain control. *Great Spirit, please.*

Once again, Urilla Wuti stepped in to strengthen
Adia's hold. The depth of the sadness, panic, and
despair was excruciating. Urilla Wuti felt Adia pull
away, knowing on some level that it was causing
pain, but then Adia reached deeper into herself and
hung on. It was taking all Urilla Wuti had to keep
from being consumed along with the younger
Healer.

It was a place of no place, of unbearable bleakness. The sense of hopelessness spread out in all directions like an inky, endless, and unrelenting void.

Then, shored up by Urilla's presence, Adia joined the consciousness of Khon'Tor with that of Tehya. And in that moment, each knew everything about the other.

Tehya experienced Khon'Tor's deep love for her. She knew his true regret and repentance for the crimes he had committed. She felt his shame, and struggle, and then the worst of it, his belief that she would be better off without him. Cold, icy threads of anguish spread through her soul and drowned both her and Adia in Khon'Tor's boundless despair and self-hatred.

And Khon'Tor's consciousness merged with Tehya. He experienced her utter lack of judgment toward him that embodied a love purer and more abiding than anyone deserved. Her heartbreak at seeing him punished, each lash ripping into her as deeply as it had sliced his flesh, the blood that dripped from his wounds, and the tears wept by her soul at his suffering becoming one. Her sense of helplessness at not being able to stop it, and her torment at not wanting to live without him, yet not being prepared to leave Arismae.

Going deeper, deeper than she had ever gone before, Adia surrounded them both and moved them all closer together. Urilla Wuti tightened her hold on Adia lest she lose herself completely in the unbearable pain of two hearts unable to bear their anguish. Adia heard Urilla Wuti's soul speaking to her, "*Let go, come back. It is too dangerous. Adia*—" But she went still farther until the crushing, empty darkness threatened to swallow them all, drown them in a bottomless sea of suffering, with only the spark of Adia and of Tehya's love as anchors to what remained of their life force.

At that moment, Urilla Wuti lost her hold on Adia, and her consciousness snapped back into her own body. Her eyes flew open, "Oh no," she cried out.

Acaraho turned and slammed his fists into the wall, and small pieces of stone flew off and scattered across the floor. In his anguish, he let out a wail that filled the halls outside the room they were in. Tears spilled down Nadiwani's cheeks as she saw the color drain from Urilla Wuti's face.

"I have lost them; I have lost them all. He is so strong and his darkness, his suffering is—truly unspeakable." Broken, Urilla Wuti buried her face in her hands.

Everything with E'ranale in the Corridor was beautiful, uplifting, and underpinned by that feeling of love and that abiding presence. However, where Adia found herself now was just the opposite. Everywhere and nowhere, there was only despair. Her soul was not strong enough to resist the tide of suffering that swelled and surrounded them all. It was dark with no sense of form—a pulsing swelling sea of hopelessness that was also swallowing her last spark of hope. Khon'Tor's suffering was so great; he was beyond understanding that he was taking both Adia and his beloved Tehya with him to his self-imposed krell.

And then the tiniest thread of light appeared. It lay in contrast to the thick blackness that permeated everything, and it was the most beautiful thing Adia had ever seen. More than anything, she wanted that light. Her soul begged, stretched, desperately reached out to it, and then slowly, from the depths of suffering and nothingness, Adia felt herself becoming more buoyant, rising out of the smothering weight of hopelessness. Something was pulling her. Something had entered the Connection and was showing her the way back.

Adia felt herself start to reassemble, once again becoming herself. Somehow, she had succeeded. She had survived the Connection, and united Khon'Tor and Tehya in a way that allowed no separation, no secrets, no fears of what the other truly felt. But would it be enough? Would Khon'Tor choose life with Tehya, or would he let her love for him pull her the rest of the way into eternal suffering?

Slowly, Adia's awareness of her physical form and her own identity returned, and she opened her eyes. It took her a moment to remember where she was, what they were doing there. When she had adjusted, she quickly looked to one side of her and then the other.

Weakly, Adia tried to prop herself up. She looked over at Acaraho. Her love. Her rock. He was standing in the corner of the room, slumped against the wall, blood welling from his scraped hands in which his head rested.

Urilla Wuti felt the sleeping mat move, and her eyes flew open. "You are here. You are back. Oh, dear Mother, I thought we had lost you."

Hearing Urilla Wuti's voice, Acaraho turned to look at his mate. She reached out to him, and he was with her in seconds, catching her up into his arms, burying his face in her neck, rocking her.

"We are leaving," he snarled as the memory of his fear took over. "I am taking her to our quarters." Adia wrapped her arms around his neck and held on tight.

"We may still need her," said Nadiwani.

"No. It is over. Adia has done enough," and he turned, ready to whisk her away.

"Acaraho, wait," Urilla Wuti called out.

He only partially turned back to her.

With great effort, Urilla Wuti rose from her position at the end of the sleeping mat and came over to them.

She placed one hand on Adia's belly and one on her head, closing her own eyes. Then she moved one hand up to rest over Adia's heart. Exhausted and spent, Adia peered at her from half-open lids.

Urilla Wuti looked at Adia, "You are both fine. You just need to rest. Let your mate minister to you, and I will be by later to check on you."

Believing the physical contact would help, Nadi-wani had carefully moved Tehya back up against Khon'Tor. The moment their bodies touched, Khon'Tor had surfaced enough to throw an arm around Tehya and pull her into him. Even though she still seemed asleep, Tehya had instinctively curled herself up into his embrace. For the first time since his collapse, Khon'Tor was resting peacefully, his breath even and unlabored. And Tehya lay as relaxed as he was.

Nodding toward the two curled up together, Urilla Wuti said to Acaraho, "I believe she may have saved them both. They are joined together now, no longer suffering alone in their own isolated krells."

Acaraho nodded at her before turning and carrying Adia away.

That evening, Tehya woke, and though she said nothing, signed for Arismae and some food. After she had eaten, she nursed her daughter as best she could, though she was still very weak.

Finally, that evening, the fever broke, and Khon'Tor woke up. He had also not eaten for days, but he had enough bodyweight to sustain him. He looked around the room, and then to his side, at his beloved Tehya.

She waited for his gaze to meet hers and then whispered, "Adoeete." She leaned over him and placed her hands on his face.

"Saraste'." Khon'Tor struggled to sit up. He ran his hand through his hair.

"I had a horrible dream, my love," said Tehya. "I was searching for you. Oh, such darkness. Hopelessness. I knew you were there but just out of reach; we were lost together, drowning in unbearable hopelessness. Then Adia helped me find you, and I wrapped my love around you, around us both, and now here we are. I love you so."

"I know. More than I have ever known anything, I know you do." He continued, "I had the oddest experience. A dream too, I imagine, one I have never experienced before and hope never to experience again. I do not remember much of it, but in this dream, I wanted to die, and then you were with me, and I realized that if I died, I would take your life with mine, and I suddenly wanted to live again. And though I cannot explain it, I now know that you truly do love me, and you do forgive me. I no longer want to die; I want to live my life, whatever is left of it, with you and Arismae."

Tehya cried and clung to him, her tears of relief dampening his hair.

When she had calmed down, Khon'Tor turned to Nadiwani and Urilla Wuti, who were still in the room and asked, "How long have I been unconscious?"

"Five days. We almost lost you, Khon'Tor." Nadiwani did not disclose that they had also almost lost Tehya.

She then turned to Urilla Wuti, "I will stay here with them; there is every reason to believe that both will fully recover, but I feel better being close by. I am comfortable, so please go and get some rest. You look exhausted."

Over the next few days, Khon'Tor's wounds began healing, and his strength slowly returned. Urilla Wuti had not visited them but had sent word that she was all right. The other High Council members were told that Khon'Tor was expected to make a full recovery, but they made no move to visit him.

Back in their quarters, Acaraho had devoted himself to Adia as much as possible. Nadiwani taught him how to make a soothing lavender tea to help Adia relax. Mapiya was already fast friends with the females of Amara, and he enlisted her help to bring Adia her favorite things to eat. Mostly he lay with her and caressed her, sometimes gently rubbing her belly.

"You seem very due to deliver," he said, noticing how ripe she was.

"I feel that I am, Acaraho. I did not want to deliver our son here, but there seems no other choice. I need Urilla Wuti and Nadiwani, and we cannot take them away from Khon'Tor and Tehya, who are in no shape to travel." As she said the words, she wondered what would become of them.

The next day, though he hated to tear himself away from Adia, Acaraho asked for a High Council meeting.

"Khon'Tor is recovering," he said, "and so is his mate, Tehya. Adia looks as if she could deliver our offspring at any moment. Since she will need the services of Urilla Wuti, and maybe Nadiwani, I request that for the moment, they all remain here and that the investigation into the second victim is suspended."

"Should Urilla Wuti leave, Iella is here," offered Harak'Sar, referring to Urilla Wuti's niece, who was now considered a Healer as well. "But I do understand your wanting a more experienced Healer to be present."

Harak'Sar, Lesharo'Mok, and Risik'Tar exchanged glances and nodded.

"We have to agree," said Lesharo'Mok. "It falls to Urilla Wuti to travel to the Deep Valley to talk to the other female, but Adia's situation is more pressing. Unfortunately, whoever it is has suffered in silence this long and will have to bear the pain a while longer."

"I will travel with Urilla Wuti when the time comes; I need to visit my people, but I will stay far away from the investigation," continued Lesharo'Mok.

"There is also the matter of returning to Kthama," said Acaraho. "My messengers have returned saying that the other Sarnonn group has not caused any trouble. Neither were any of the Brothers harmed or threatened, just as Haan, the Sarnonn Leader, predicted. He has been talking with the rebel group, and it appears the hostility has truly abated. They are talking of a future where the two factions are reunited at Kht'shWea."

Harak'Sar raised his eyebrows, "The other Sarnonn will be moving into Kthama Minor?"

"Yes," said Acaraho. "I know, you are concerned that this means more Sarnonn next door to us. But I know Haan; he would not allow it if he were not sure they have no more designs on Kthama or intention to attack us. There is no need. Kht'shWea offers every-thing Kthama does. Also, the message from Straf'Tor was very clear. It appears they have had a change of heart. I believe that Tarnor was the driving force behind it all, and with him removed, the emotions have righted themselves."

"Cut the head off the Sarius snake," said Risik'-

Tar, almost to himself, repeating the ancient adage on how to beat a more powerful enemy.

"Exactly," said Acaraho. "I will leave you now and start making plans for our people to begin returning to Kthama. We will never forget your hospitality."

"Keep us posted, Adik'Tar Acaraho. Until we can find a permanent solution, you are now Kthama's Leader," said Harak'Sar.

Acaraho frowned. "When was this decided? I do not want to be the Leader of the High Rocks or any other community. I do not have Khon'Tor's drive, or any desire for it. Nor am I qualified. I am not of 'Tor descent. I am willing to serve temporarily, but as far as I am concerned, the sooner this is resolved, the better."

As Acaraho walked away, Lesharo'Mok said, "He does not see himself clearly. He has always been a leader. When he looks at his reflection, he sees only Khon'Tor's shadow."

"Let us get Kthama's people back to their home," said Risik'Tar. "After that, we will discuss how best to proceed. By then, hopefully, the Sarnonn will be fully reconciled, and the balance of Khon'Tor's punishment will be decided. Once those fall into place, we can pull the larger High Council back together."

Harak'Sar frowned. "We still need somehow to resolve the matter of bloodlines. We still have the two options—breed with the Sarnonn, or somehow, though it seems impossible, bring in Waschini seed.

But the first matter is to announce that Khon'Tor is no longer the Leader of the High Rocks and that the High Protector will serve in the interim."

"And just how are we going to slip that by them without answering the larger question of why?" scoffed Risik'Tar. "Why would such a powerful Leader as Khon'Tor simply step aside? His crimes cannot be revealed without inciting the civil war Adia has spent her life trying to prevent. We must come up with a plausible reason; we owe her that much. And there is the issue of Kurak'Kahn. I sense there is more to it than what he said, but he can no longer serve on the High Council, let alone as Overseer. So we need to appoint another Overseer as well."

"There is still a third victim," pointed out Lesharo'Mok.

The three Leaders nodded their agreement and fell silent. Their faces were lined from the strain of the growing list of serious problems.

"We can do nothing to help the third female," sighed Harak'Sar. "But I agree with you, Risik'Tar. There is more to Kurak'Kahn's story. I suggest we find out now before something else jumps up to bite us."

The population of the High Rocks that had been dispersed between the Far High Hills and the Deep Valley slowly returned to Kthama. Haan had done as promised in watching over Kthama, but there had been no trouble from the former rebels and no sign of Akar'Tor. The mature females were the first to go, lending their services to get the wheels of the community moving again before the younger females, offspring, and Elders set out.

Life and order returned to the community of the High Rocks. Under the oversight of First Guard Awan, Kthama was once again filled with activity. And though on the surface everything seemed to have returned to normal, it was not the same, and everyone felt it.

The strain of what had occurred ran like an undercurrent through all the daily activities. Though life returned to normal, the People were reserved, quiet. The offspring did not run carefree through the communal rooms. The females' happy chatter did not fill the air. And conspicuously absent was their leadership—Khon'Tor, Tehya, the High Protector Acaraho, and their beloved Healer, Adia.

There was no explanation for their failure to return with the others, and rumors started to threaten the fragile security that the community had rediscovered in returning home.

It was time for Nadiwani to return to Kthama.

"I do not want to leave you, Adia," she protested.

"You must. Kthama cannot be without any

medical assistance. With us both here, what if something were to happen? We have young mothers needing guidance, and Elders who are exhausted from their travel here and back."

"You are about to deliver. How can I not be here for you, my dear friend?"

"I know. I also want you here," Adia had replied. "But despite how we feel, you and I both know that you must return ahead of me. Even though Oh'Dar and Ithua could assist, Kthama needs you there."

And so the two long-time friends had embraced, and Nadiwani prepared for her return to her people.

The Sarnonn at Kht'shWea had made great progress in their efforts to duplicate the People's leadership and community structures. Haan had met many times with Dorn and his followers and was satisfied that their transformation was genuine. He had allowed them to move into Kht'shWea. Dorn had surprisingly turned out to be very influential with his group; Straf'Tor's manifestation had certainly sealed the deal for the turnaround. The reward of living at Kht'shWea had reinforced an atmosphere of unity. The females, in particular, were very grateful for the convenience of the Mother Stream running through the depths of the cave system. The fresh air, easy water supply, and vast expanse of living quarters had raised everyone's spirits. If anyone mourned Tarnor, it was in secret.

At their request, the new Guardians were allowed to move together into one of the sequestered tunnel branches, though Haan noticed that they made frequent trips to the surface for meetings. Whether it was a need for solitude or the call of the crystalized stones that had been transformed when they were, he did not know. He gave them their privacy, but there was a limit to how much segregation from the larger community he would be comfortable with.

Thord and Lellaach had become the Leaders of the new Guardians. Haan knew them both well and was not alarmed. They had been paired for some time, though they had no offspring. Upon reflection, Haan realized that none of the paired Guardians had yet produced offspring. He wondered if that were just a coincidence or if a larger hand had been at play.

One day, Haan headed to Kthama to meet with Khon'Tor and the High Protector. When he arrived and asked for them, he was greeted by First Guard Awan.

"Are Khon'Tor and the High Protector still not available?"

"They have still not returned to Kthama, Adik'Tar Haan. I do not know when they will, either, and I am officially in charge. What help can I provide you with?"

Haan shook his head and looked off in the

distance. The increasing force of the magnetic waves from the vortex below Kthama were a constant and growing distraction, and he paused to listen to them. He returned his gaze and studied Awan's face. *Does he not feel it?* "Do the Akassa navigate by the magnetic forces that flow through Etera?"

Awan was caught off guard at the unusual question.

"Yes, we do. Some of us are more sensitive to them than others. These are usually those who find themselves called to be watchers, as they can more easily navigate the areas surrounding Kthama without relying on visual cues."

Haan nodded. "And do you not feel a strong swell of currents stirring below Kthama?"

"I have felt a change, Adik'Tar Haan. Only I do not perhaps perceive the difference as strongly as it seems you do."

After a pause, Haan said, "When Khon'Tor and the High Protector return, please tell them I would like to meet with them."

Awan nodded and watched the Sarnonn leave. As he was standing there, Nadiwani approached.

"Have you heard anything about Adia's condition?"

He looked down at her, for the first time noticing how attractive she was. He blinked and tilted his head as if taking another look.

"Is something wrong?"

"No. It is just—something I just noticed— Never

mind. No, I have not heard from anyone. I imagine it is hard for you to be here—with your friend so close to delivering her offspring."

Nadiwani sighed and then remarked with a grin, "I should not say this, First Guard Awan, but you are quite insightful."

Awan chuckled, a rare break from his usual stoic demeanor. "Perhaps there is more to me than meets the eye, Helper."

"So I am beginning to wonder," and Nadiwani's lips quirked. "Please let me know the moment you hear anything," she added.

"Of course," he replied, bowing slightly.

As she walked away, she turned back to take another look and caught him watching her leave.

Nadiwani returned to the Healer's Quarters. With Adia gone, she had taken to staying there. She knew Adia would not mind, and it made her feel closer to her friend to be in the surroundings in which they had spent so much time together.

What I would give to know what is going on now back at the Far High Hills. Our people have been through so much; how are the remaining Leaders going to tell them that Khon'Tor is no longer the Leader of the High Rocks? And Adia sacrificed and suffered for decades to avoid just this type of outcome. Without an heir, there is no one to take over the leadership of Kthama. In all our known history, this has never happened; how will the High Council solve this dilemma?

Just then, Nootau came looking for her. "Have you heard anything about my mother?"

"No. I am sorry. There is no word."

"It is time for me to return to her."

Nadiwani thought for a moment. "You have only just arrived back here, but I think that is a great idea. I know your mother would be very happy to see you. And your brother is due at any moment. You could be one of the first to welcome him into Etera."

"I do not mind the walk from Kthama to Far High Hills. It clears my head. And, I am going to help name him."

Nadiwani smiled at his enthusiasm. Then out of curiosity, she asked, "What *would* you name him?"

"Something unusual. Perhaps a name we have never heard before. There is going to be something special about him," and Nootau's voice became wistful.

Nadiwani cocked her head, nagged by a stray thought from the back of her mind. *He speaks with confidence about that, almost with a Healer's knowing.*

"Tell the First Guard and Mapiya before you go. We do not need sentries out looking for you."

"I will. I will also give your love to everyone at the Far High Hills."

Nadiwani smiled. *He is so gentle of spirit, nothing like his father. He would have been a great Leader—in the vein of Adia's father, Apenimom'Mok, I think. Luckily, he does not crave authority, for if he did and ever found he was robbed of his rightful heritage, someone in his position could easily become bitter.*

Khon'Tor's wounds had finally healed enough that he could resume regular activities. Only, having been stripped of leadership, he was at a loss as to what those activities might be. Tehya had tended to his wounds without fail, applying the healing anointments that Urilla Wuti had supplied.

"Your wounds are healing up nicely, Adoeete," she said one evening as she spread the rest of the day's dose across his back. "But I fear there will still be some scarring."

"It will raise questions, I am sure," he said. Though the matter was not to be discussed outside of the High Council, for the sakes of Tehya and Arismae, Khon'Tor was worried that the information would somehow leak out.

"I wonder what is going on at Kthama. I am sure you also do."

"It is on my mind. But I am no longer the Leader. I must let go of it all, somehow."

Tehya stopped spreading the ointment for a moment, and Khon'Tor turned to face her.

"I was not done," she exclaimed.

"It is enough. Thank you."

"Adoeete," Tehya said softly. "We will find a way

to make a life for ourselves. Harak'Sar has offered us sanctuary. And my parents are here, and they adore Arismae. But you, what of your happiness? Being Adik'Tar is not merely a role you were assigned. It is the very core of who you are. I know that better than ever since Adia— connected us."

"I cannot see much past the last remaining tasks I have to accomplish if I am able. Harak'Sar's offer is more than generous."

Khon'Tor grasped her hands in his and kissed her fingertips gently. She raised an eyebrow and smiled.

"You are feeling better," she teased.

"Arrange again for that wet nurse who helped care for Arismae, and I will show you just how much better I feel." Tehya blushed, and for a precious moment, everything felt to Khon'Tor as it had been before his downfall.

That evening Tehya and Khon'Tor set aside all their worries and concentrated on each other. She had tended him for so long, and he wanted to take care of her now. He had asked for advice and then had one of the female helpers bring him stone bowls and preparations for him to heat some water with lavender and peppermint leaves. When it was ready, he moved the bowls to a small table and called Tehya over to him.

"Slip off your wraps, and let me look at you."

Though she had gotten more accustomed to his wanting to look at her, he could still see the color come up in her cheeks. She closed her eyes and did as he asked, letting first the top covering and then the one wrapped around her hips slide to the floor. She stepped aside and kicked both of them away.

Khon'Tor chuckled. "Open your eyes. I want you to see me looking at you."

A little sound escaped her lips, but she did as he said. They had come to an agreement in this game. He told her what to do, and she complied, though not without some resistance.

Khon'Tor let his eyes sweep over her curves. Childbirth had changed her maidenly figure in delicious ways. Though she was still a bit too thin, her hips now swelled more below her tiny waist. He let his gaze follow back up to meet hers, and without breaking contact, he dipped the soft woven cloth in the warm water and began to wash her.

She closed her eyes in pleasure as the warmth touched her skin. The material of the cloth added to the delight; the smell of lavender and peppermint soothed and relaxed her. Khon'Tor slowly made his way down her frame, frequently rinsing the cloth to ensure the water was still warm against her skin. As he ran the cloth over her, the changes in her breathing signaled her anticipation.

He rinsed the cloth again and ordered her to widen her stance. "Ohhh—" she moaned as he slipped his hand between her legs and slowly caressed her there. "Wider," he ordered. She complied and closed her eyes in pleasure.

He felt her knees give and stopped long enough to stand and scoop her up, moving her over to the sleeping mat. Knowing she was now damp from the water, he pulled a soft skin over her to keep her warm, moving it aside enough to slip between her legs and return to her most intimate area.

Before long, he felt her tense and knew the splendor was not long behind. Finally, he felt her spasm and her sweet release wash over him. Once the waves had abated, he slid up between her legs and eagerly pressed his hard shaft against her entrance. As he had once long ago on their first night together, he entered her only the least amount and then withdrew.

"Whaaa—" she murmured. "No, please, come back," she whispered.

"Come back and what, Saraste'? What is it you want of me?"

Her eyes widened as understanding dawned.

"Tell me what you want. I need to hear you say it."

"No, please. Do not make me."

He leaned forward, so his warm breath played against her ear as he whispered, "How do I know what you want unless you tell me?" He longed to hear her say it, knowing it was far outside her comfort zone—or that of any of the females—to speak so graphically.

He pressed himself the slightest bit back inside

her. But when she raised her hips to draw him farther in, he backed away.

"You must tell me what you want me to do," he repeated.

She wrapped her legs around his hips as best she could, trying to bring him closer, and he chuckled to himself. Her obvious need for him to fill her pleased him no end but also made it harder to hold back.

"Is this what you want?" he asked, pressing himself inside her again, this time a margin farther.

"Yes. Yes, please."

"Tell me. Tell me, and you can have as much of me as you can handle."

He entered her a little more and held his place. Again, she tried to raise her hips but, once again, he backed away so she could not gain any more of his length within her.

"Tell me you want me inside you, and I will give you what you want. Tell me to bury myself in you and pump all my seed into you. Ask me to *Rok* you Saraste', and I will."

She tossed her head from side to side; her burning need to be filled by his hard strength was at war with her shame at the words he wanted to have cross her lips. Words that only the males spoke— words that no female would ever utter.

"I cannot. I cannot say those things. Females do not speak so!"

"As you wish then," and he slowly began to withdraw himself from her, making sure she felt every inch of him leaving.

"You are denying me," she glared at him, brows furrowed.

"Not at all. You can have what you want. I have laid down the terms. All you have to do is meet them."

As the tip of him left her, he began pleasuring her again, his fingers quickly finding and gently circling the sensitive pearl at the top of her entrance. At the Ashwea Tare, he had been taught that females had two separate needs. It was a difficult concept for the males to understand. Females needed the release of the splendor, but there was also a need to be filled by the male, a desire for the deep satisfaction of his hardness inside her. How they could be separate was a concept the males had to accept without understanding; for them, the mating and release of the splendor were satisfied together.

Khon'Tor knew exactly how to bring Tehya to the crest and up and over into ecstasy. He also knew that even that exquisite pleasure was not a substitute for the feeling of his thick shaft filling her and making her his own. He gambled that in time her need for him to be inside her would overrule her embarrassment at saying the things he was asking to hear from her lips.

He teased her to the brink of splendor and then stopped. She snarled at him this time, "Stop teasing me. Give me what I need."

"What is it you need? Say what it is, and it is yours," and he brought her again to the crest and stopped short.

"You. I need you."

"I am right here." He was giving no ground.

"I need you to *Rok me*. There I said it. I need you to Rok me, *hard*," and with one motion, Khon'Tor was over her, then inside her, filling her and giving her the satisfaction she was wild for. He rocked her frame, and she clawed his sides, and for a few moments, they escaped the burdens of reality.

When it was over, Khon'Tor fell asleep, savoring the feeling of Tehya curled up in his arms and setting aside his worry about the future.

But his respite was short-lived. The future was about to come crashing in.

Urilla Wuti was ministering to Adia when Acaraho gingerly entered. He stood blocking the doorway. "May I interrupt?"

"Of course," Adia smiled.

"I have someone here to see you," and out from behind Acaraho stepped Nootau. Urilla Wuti smiled at seeing father and son together.

"Oh!" exclaimed Adia as Nootau rushed to embrace her. He bent down and hugged her, careful not to put pressure on her belly.

"My son, you have returned at just the right time.

As you can see, your brother has not yet entered Etera. Sit and tell me how you are doing and what is going on back home? How is Nadiwani faring? And what are you *wearing*?"

Nootau extracted himself from her embrace and sat on the sleeping mat beside her. He took a moment to search her face before continuing.

"You look well, Mama. I was not worried, and yet I was."

"I understand. But there is time before your brother arrives. So sit and tell me; what is going on at Kthama?"

"First Guard Awan and Mapiya are doing a fine job of keeping everything together. The families and the groups have settled back into their living areas, and life is returning to normal. Many of the females without young offspring are out fishing the springs. The hunting parties are also working to make sure there will be an abundance of jerky for the colder months. Even though no trouble is expected, Awan stationed extra guards around the fishing crews. But—"

Adia knew what was coming.

"Everyone is wondering where you and my father are. And also why Khon'Tor and Tehya have not returned. It cannot go on like this much longer, Mama. Someone needs to come and tell them something. What *is* going on?"

Acaraho came over and knelt by the young male whom he thought of as his son. "In time, your mother and I will return to Kthama. I do not believe Khon'Tor and Tehya will be returning. I do not have more that I can tell you, son."

"What of Oh'Dar?" asked Adia. "The messengers sent word that the Brothers were not bothered in any way by the rebel Sarnonn."

"Oh'Dar is very concerned about you. The Sarnonn did not trouble the Brothers at all, just as everyone said they would not. They did hear the crack and see the sky light up when the figure of Straf'Tor appeared. Everyone is still talking about that. But still, it is not a good time for you to be away.

"Oh'Dar has been talking to me, the two of us trying to figure out how to begin teaching everyone the skill of the Waschini writing—as Khon'Tor asked him to do. I am excited about helping him. He is calling it school. Oh, and Oh'Dar did say to please tell Khon'Tor thanks again for the wolf cub. She is keeping Snana and Noshoba busy since he and Acise are a little obsessed with their new paired status." He paused. "There is so much to tell you that I feel I am rambling!"

Adia smiled. "I was worried that day would never come for Oh'Dar. And you? How are you doing, Nootau? Sometimes stressful situations change people." She braced herself for the answer. Though he and his sister Nimida had settled into a platonic relationship, she still had fears in the back of her mind that the current might turn.

"I am still not ready, Mama. I will admit that the

Ashwea Tare piqued my interest, but I know that mating without being paired is forbidden, and there is no one in my heart who occupies my thoughts at night." He looked up and winked at his father.

Adia was pleased by the sassy nature of the wink, even though it was not directly intended for her.

"But when I do get anxious, for lack of a better word, I just do as father did before you two were paired; I uproot a lot of dead trees."

They all laughed together at that remark, even Urilla Wuti.

"Nimida, on the other hand— She and Tar seem to have taken up with each other. I guess we could see it coming; it was clear at the Ashwea Awhidi that they are getting close. I would not be surprised if they ask to be paired."

Adia did not even try to suppress a broad smile as she looked over at Acaraho.

"That pleases us both greatly. Thank you for telling us," Acaraho replied.

"And as for this hide I am wearing," continued Nootau, "do you remember the speech Khon'Tor gave at the pairing ceremony? He spoke of the significance of the three of us, the Sarnonn, the People, and the Brothers being united. Well, I decided it was a way to bring further unity between our people and the Brothers. I do not know if it will catch on with the other males, but now that I am used to it, I rather fancy it. Quite a few of the younger ones have started following my lead."

Nootau paused and looked at his mother quietly. "I can see you are tired."

"I will come with you and let your mother rest," replied Acaraho, and they left the two Healers to themselves.

Adia asked Urilla Wuti for that day's news of Khon'Tor.

"His wounds are healing, and Tehya is taking care of him. I checked on them recently, but it may all be for nothing—"

"I know. The female he accosted at the Deep Valley. Where I grew up—" and Adia's voice trailed off.

"Yes, I fear I must travel there soon—yet frankly, with Nadiwani being at Kthama, I do not want to leave you. I must be here for my conscience; I would never forgive myself if anything happened to you or the offspring."

"Is there something you are not telling me?" Adia had instantly become agitated at the slightest hint of a problem. "You did not tell me I was carrying twins before, for fear of upsetting me. Please, *do not keep anything from me again*. The last time you scanned him, you told me everything was fine. And in the Corridor, E'ranale also said there was nothing wrong."

"He is healthy; I sense no cause for alarm. If there is something else going on, it is being hidden from me."

"What do you mean, Urilla Wuti, hidden from

you? Did something happen when I went to the Connection to unite Tehya and Khon'Tor? Did something change then?"

"No, but we have not spoken about that experience. It is time we discuss what happened."

Adia lay back on the sleeping mat and tried to calm herself. Then she told Urilla Wuti what she had experienced.

"I felt some of this with you, Adia," Urilla Wuti interrupted. "I also felt incredible anguish, both physical and mental, at the depths of the Connection. And then suddenly you were gone—all three of you. Somehow my connection with you broke, and I was thrown back into the reality of Etera. I thought you were lost forever."

"If someone had not pulled me back," Adia said softly, "I would not have been able to stop myself from giving in."

"E'ranale. E'ranale saved you and brought the three of you back here," whispered Urilla Wuti.

"No," Adia said softly. "No. It was not E'ranale. It was a consciousness I had never experienced before. So powerful. So much more powerful even than E'ranale. There are no words to describe it. Whoever it was brought me back with as little effort as it would take me to fold this bed cover over. And she must also have created a way for Khon'Tor and Tehya to find their way back. But from what you have said, it does not sound as if either Khon'Tor or Tehya remember much of it. From my experience with

Connections, Tehya should have learned the truth about Nimida and Nootau, yet she appears not to have retained any details."

Adia saw the tension growing in Urilla Wuti's face as the older Healer bit her lip, perhaps to keep from interrupting again.

Finally, after a moment of silence, Adia continued. "As I was about to break back through to Etera, I sensed a name. Oh, Urilla Wuti, you are the only one I can truly trust to believe me."

Urilla waited for it.

"*Pan.*"

CHAPTER 7

Lesharo'Mok, Harak'Sar, and Risik'Tar had assembled once again.

"We need an answer from the second victim—the female of my community. Until we get past that, we cannot announce Khon'Tor's status," stated Lesharo'Mok.

"We have already discussed this. Urilla Wuti needs to stay here until Adia delivers her offspring," pointed out Risik'Tar.

"But, the longer it takes, the more rumors will spread about Khon'Tor's absence at the High Rocks."

"It cannot be helped," said Harak'Sar. "But it is only a day's journey to the Deep Valley, and another back. I will check with Urilla Wuti and see if she thinks she can leave Adia for a few days. If nothing else, though, we need to remind High Protector Acaraho that he will be stepping in as Leader of the

High Rocks. At least until we can find another solution."

"Let us look for him now. There is no benefit in waiting on that."

The three males found Acaraho speaking once again with Thorak.

"May we have a word with you, Commander?" asked Harak'Sar, dismissing his own High Protector.

"We must speak with you about the situation with the High Rocks. Come and sit with us," added Risik'Tar.

Acaraho followed them to a small, secluded meeting room and watched with growing interest as Harak'Sar pulled the stone door closed.

Lesharo'Mok spoke first. "It appears that Khon'Tor will survive his wounds, but there is still the matter of the victim at the Deep Valley. We are waiting for your offspring to be delivered. As soon as possible afterward, Urilla Wuti must travel there to determine what punishment the second female will decide on."

"If he survives that punishment, then we will have to announce the disposition of his leadership and give a plausible explanation for his stepping down," said Harak'Sar.

Acaraho was relieved to hear that they had not changed their minds about revealing Khon'Tor's crimes. Urilla Wuti was right; nothing good would come of it for the victims, who, if they had wanted their stories revealed, would have come forward before this.

"As far as the High Rocks is concerned, we have decided you must assume permanent leadership," added Risik'Tar.

Acaraho almost lost his steely composure.

"I do not wish to lead the High Rocks. And I am not of Khon'Tor's bloodline; I am not qualified. I agreed to lead temporarily."

Risik'Tar shook his head. "As there is no one in Khon'Tor's bloodline other than the female Arismae, we must make an exception to the rule. As soon as you and your mate are ready to return to Kthama, we will be calling a meeting to announce it."

"I must discuss this with Adia. It also affects her."

"You are forgetting, Commander. This appointment is not something that can be refused," Harak'Sar stated.

Acaraho exhaled, nodded, and excused himself to find Adia.

Adia was in their borrowed quarters, resting on the sleeping mat.

"You look uncomfortable," Acaraho said to his mate, who was curled on her side with part of the sleeping mat bunched up under her belly.

"I am," she said, lifting her head long enough to look at him. "But, so do you; what has happened?"

"I have just come from meeting with Lesharo'Mok, Risik'Tar, and Harak'Sar. They are appointing me Leader of the High Rocks."

Adia looked up again at Acaraho, "And you do not want to be."

"No, I do not. I have never wanted that kind of leadership. I am content with directing the guards and watchers and coordinating the other male tasks. Besides, I am not of his bloodline, though I know they have to make an exception. Perhaps First Guard Awan—"

Adia sat up with difficulty. "I know you do not want this. You are not driven by power like Khon'Tor was. But a Leader does not need great ambition to lead greatly. My father was the perfect example. You are the best choice. Sometimes those who want least to lead are the most qualified. I have long believed you would make a great Leader of the High Rocks.

"First Guard Awan would not accept it," Adia continued. "He defers to you. He would never be comfortable out from under your direction."

Acaraho covered his chin with his hand and paced a short distance.

"It would make you both Second and Third Rank," he pointed out as he turned back to her.

"If the High Council can appoint you Leader, they can determine a Third Rank in this case. Perhaps Nadiwani, though she is not a Healer."

Adia started to get up, but Acaraho came over and sat next to her.

"Here, lean on me," and he sat next to the wall and let her recline against him.

"Oooh. Thank you. That is much better. My love, things are changing, whether we like it or not. We have been through so much in just the past few years. Change has always been hard for the People, and I know everyone has been pushed to the limit. But this is one change I do not believe anyone will have a hard time accepting. Perhaps at first, but everyone recognizes your abilities, and most importantly, your dedication to Kthama. Part of it will depend on how the High Council explains it," she offered.

As she finished speaking, she let out a moan and placed her hand on her belly. "It is drawing close; please go and find Urilla Wuti. Our offspring is about to make his appearance."

Acaraho stepped out and quickly returned with Urilla Wuti and her aides. Iella and Nitika immediately began making the final preparations for the area where the birthing stone had been placed, spreading leaves and other absorbent material below it, and padding the rock itself with several soft skins. Acaraho left to wait outside, as he had done decades ago when Nootau and Nimida were delivered.

Before long, Adia's water broke.

Nitika took a position behind Adia, supporting her as she leaned back. As with the first delivery, Urilla Wuti knelt before her ready to catch the tiny offspring and guide him gently into the soft padding bundled below.

What seemed like forever did not take as long as it felt, and soon Adia was pushing with all her might. Then, with a final shout from his mother, the offspring was there. Adia once again heard the healthy cry of a son, this time one she had not been ordered by the High Council to give up.

Deep underground Kthama and Kht'shWea, the magnetic currents of Etera flared again. The Sarnonn Guardians all looked at each other in surprise.

Haan and Haaka were just finishing up the evening meal when Haan stopped eating. "Did you feel that?" he asked Haaka.

"Yes. I wonder what is going on?"

"I do not know," replied Haan, making a mental note to speak with the Guardians and see if they had also felt it. "The currents have lately been active everywhere. There is always ebb and flow within the vortex, but I have never before experienced so strong a surge."

He pushed away his remaining food and rose. "I am going to find Thord."

The Guardian Leader was in the meadow above Kht'shWea. From the look on his face, Haan could tell that Thord was expecting him.

"You are going to ask me what that was, and I do

not know," began Thord. "But it was something significant. It feels as if a massive influx of Aezaiteria has entered our realm, but what it is—that is being withheld from me. When the time is right, it will be made known."

"Others will also have felt it. I dislike not having answers."

"I sense no cause for alarm, Haan." Thord changed the subject. "Is there any word on the Leader of the High Rocks?"

"No. First Guard Awan is in charge. I am confident that if there were any news, he would have sent a messenger."

"Khon'Tor and his mate, and the High Protector, and the Healer, Adia—they have been away a long time. I find it unusual, especially considering what just took place. There must be something seriously wrong or extremely important for them not to have returned to their people at Kthama."

Kayerm was empty. Its silence was broken only by the faint scurry of lizards scared from their hiding places in the crevices. Akar'Tor looked around. He walked down the hallway to the living quarters where he had grown up with his mother and Haan. He touched the hide curtain and scuffed a few stray rocks away from the center of the room.

Everything is gone. Everything I knew, everyone who

loved me—or at least said they did. Even Inhrah has deserted me, gone to live with Haan and the others. Tarnor is dead—I could not care less; he deserved it. Dorn deserted the cause the moment Tarnor fell. The Sassen have abandoned me, and I do not know how to make it on my own. But before I die, I will make someone pay. At least then they will not forget me.

Akule and Kayah had returned home to Kthama. Akule was filled with guilt over what had happened to his mate, blaming himself for not turning in Khon'Tor when he suspected it was he who had attacked and assaulted Adia. If his relationship with Kayah had been stilted before, now it was nearly unbearable.

Akule noticed a shift in Kayah the moment they returned to Kthama.

Alone in their quarters for the first time since she had been evacuated, Kayah sat on the sleeping mat, eyes downcast.

"Where do we go from here?" Akule asked, standing a few feet away.

"I do not know. I expect you will ask for Bak'tah-Awhidi," she said quietly.

'Why would you think that?"

"I deceived you. I hid the truth from you all these years. And our pairing has not been even mildly satisfactory, far less than what you hoped for, I know."

"Is that what you want—Bak'tah-Awhidi?" he asked.

"I do not know what I want, just that I do not want to go on living like this. You would have a chance to find happiness with someone else—and you have grounds."

Akule walked away and turned his back for a moment. Then he returned and sat next to her.

"Kayah, surely you do not believe that I blame you in any way for what Khon'Tor did to you, or for not telling me? You are innocent. And I understand why you did not come forward. He was the Leader of the very community of the male you were paired to. Who would you tell? I cannot imagine what you have been through all this time."

"I cannot be the mate you want me to be."

Akule took her hands in his. "No. You cannot."

Kayah winced, and Akule immediately regretted causing the hurt he saw in her eyes.

"What I meant is, you cannot while we are here. No one could. It is too much to ask of anyone. But perhaps, somewhere else—"

"I do not understand. Are you saying you would leave Kthama?"

"I love you, Kayah. Despite all our troubles. Perhaps somewhere else, perhaps back at your home, the Far High Hills, you could find peace and happiness again, and your parents are there. Yes, I would leave Kthama if it would help you find peace."

Kayah threw her arms around his neck. "Oh. It never occurred to me you might leave here on my behalf. You have been so patient, Akule. Far more than I could have expected. I am so sorry for all the wasted years."

"We are still young. We have lots of time. Let us make a new start and see if we can find our way through this together."

"But would you be able to be a watcher there? You do not know their land as you do here."

"Something will work out. What is important is that we try. I was a watcher because the solitary lifestyle fit my bachelor status at the time. I am a good hunter and a fairly good toolmaker. I will find some way to contribute."

"How soon could we leave?"

"Let me talk to Awan, and I will let you know. I am sure some arrangements have to be made with the Leader there."

"Harak'Sar. Yes."

Harak'Sar received the message and sent for Acaraho. He immediately asked after Adia.

"I have not seen much of you since Adia had the offspring. How are they?"

"They are fine. Adia is just taking some time for

herself. The last year has been long and exhausting in many ways."

"Everyone is asking; when do we get to meet your offspring?"

"I am not sure. We need some privacy right now."

Harak'Sar nodded and moved on to business. "I have received a request from one of your watchers, Akule. He is the mate of one of Khon'Tor's victims, the female Kayah, who ordered the fifty lashes. They returned to Kthama but have found it unbearable for her to live there. They are asking to be accepted here."

"That creates a serious problem since you have given Khon'Tor asylum here."

"Yes. The only solution I have is for the announcement to be made about Khon'Tor stepping down from the leadership of the High Rocks. And that you are taking over. Perhaps that will provide her the needed relief. I doubt she will want to come here knowing that Khon'Tor will now be here. That is, depending on the judgment from the second victim."

"It all comes down to that, then. So, you called me here to ask if Urilla Wuti and I are ready to travel to the Deep Valley?"

"Yes, I did."

"I will immediately speak with her about when we can leave."

Acaraho returned to their quarters to speak with Adia.

"Harak'Sar wants me and Urilla Wuti to go to the Deep Valley to speak with the other victim. Will you be all right if we leave?" he asked.

"Yes. We will be fine. Iella will assist me if I need anything," she said. Her heart was heavy. *Will this all be for naught? Are we bringing Khon'Tor back from the brink of death only to be ready to face another punishment from the second victim? But it has to be done. We can no longer knowingly leave another soul suffering in silence from Khon'Tor's crimes.*

Acaraho saw the sorrow creep over Adia's face.

"How can you still feel compassion for Khon'-Tor?" he asked. "Perhaps it was one thing when we believed he attacked you out of a state of madness, but to know he intentionally took others Without Their Consent?"

"It is difficult to understand. Part of it is my calling, I think—it is not given to judge others, only to care for those in need. Part of it is concern and sympathy for Tehya. She has done no wrong, yet her life is being dragged through this turmoil with him. And Arismae, what will become of her?

"I am relieved that no one wishes to make this public. You know that was my belief all along, that nothing will change what has happened, and as long as the victims wish for anonymity, only harm would come of bringing it to light. Sometimes there are no easy answers. If he had truly not changed, it would be easier to hate him and let it go at that."

"I made peace with what he did to you because that was what you wanted," said Acaraho. "I even called him friend. But this—knowing he was in his right mind when he committed these other crimes—for this, I do not believe I can find forgiveness. Even for your sake, Saraste'."

"I cannot ask you to be less than who you are, my love. I understand. I did not immediately arrive at my current feelings; I have had my own struggles ever since it happened. Forgiveness is a journey, not a destination. It is not achieved in one moment. It is not a single point in time at which one arrives; at least it has not been for me. When my anger resurfaces, I have to work to let it go, trusting that everything will work together for good, no matter how painful it may be at that moment. If I had known he had committed this atrocity against other females, would I have made the same choice? Yes, after much reflection, I believe I would have. Each one has to find her own way through."

Acaraho remained silent.

Adia continued, "I will await your return. Once we know the outcome of this last piece, then we will know the next step."

Acaraho drew Adia to him, kissed her, and then left to find Urilla Wuti.

Acaraho and Urilla Wuti spoke little on the journey, each lost in their own thoughts. When they were close, Lesharo'Mok's watcher alerted the Leader that they were coming.

Lesharo'Mok, who had only returned to the Deep Valley a few days earlier, greeted them in the entrance with a female at his side. His High Protector, Teirac, was also there. After introducing Teirac, he introduced the female. "This is Tar'sa. Tar'sa is one of our head females. She takes care of our guests, and she will show you to your quarters. We have located you near to each other. She will also be available to provide any special assistance you need, either of you."

Neither Acaraho nor Urilla Wuti acknowledged that it was Tar'sa was with whom they had come to speak.

"We will only be staying a few days, I am sure," said Acaraho. "Thank you in advance for your hospitality, Lesharo'Mok."

"We are pleased to have you here, Commander. And of course, everyone knows of the legend, Urilla Wuti."

Urilla Wuti placed her hands on her cheeks to cover the color she felt rising. "Oh, I do not know that I am a legend, Adik'Tar 'Mok. But thank you for the compliment. It *was* a compliment, correct?"

They chuckled, and Tar'sa led them to their quarters. On the way, she pointed out the common eating area, assembly rooms, and general layout.

"Your water gourds are filled. I will return with some food and then let you rest. You must be tired from your trip. I am sorry about the door to your quarters, Healer," she said to Urilla Wuti. "I can see that it will be difficult for you to open and close,"

"It can stay ajar. I am not concerned for my safety."

"No one will enter your quarters without your permission or invitation, I assure you of that," said Tar'sa.

Acaraho adjusted the door to Urilla Wuti's liking and followed Tar'sa down to his space.

"If you would like to join us for the common meal, let me know. I will bring something for now and then check later. If you prefer to eat your evening meal here, I can have it brought to you."

"Thank you. You seem to enjoy your position here," observed Acaraho.

"I do. I meet so many interesting people, and I have a heart for making others feel welcome. I will be back shortly."

Acaraho was not particularly tired, but they had no reason to be there other than to speak with the female who had just left, and the less noticeable their visit was, the better. He went back up the tunnel and from outside her room called out to Urilla Wuti.

"You may enter, Commander."

Acaraho squeezed through the partially opened door.

"When do you think it proper to speak with Tar'sa?"

"I will have to speak to her alone. It will depend on when the time feels right. Probably tomorrow. I do not want to rush it, but I am also aware of your discomfort in leaving your mate and offspring."

"Urilla—" he said, using the informal version of her name and suddenly wanting to know. "Why do you think our offspring—"

"I know, Commander. I do not have answers for you. But I believe there is someone who does. Adia and I will contact her; I have just been giving Adia time with the offspring until she is ready to accept the answers."

"You are speaking of E'ranale?"

"Yes. She will know what all of it means."

"We cannot continue to keep our offspring in hiding. People are wondering."

"There are answers. We just have to search for them."

"I will leave you then, and unless something urgent happens, we will speak later."

The next morning, Tar'sa checked in with Urilla Wuti first. "Did you sleep properly?"

"I did, thank you. The sleeping mat was particularly comfortable."

"Because of the terrain, we have an ample supply of bedding materials."

"It is lush here; I have always thought so. Tell me about yourself, Tar'sa. Do you have a family?"

"I am paired, yes. We do not have offspring. It just never happened, but we still have time. My mate is a good male. He is a good provider."

"We are only staying a short while. I want to explain to you why we are here."

"It is none of my business; you do not need to explain anything to me," Tar'sa replied.

"I do, though. Because the reason we are here is to speak with you."

"Me? I am no one of consequence. Why would you wish to speak with me?"

"Acaraho is the High Protector of the High Rocks. The Leader of the High Rocks is Khon'Tor. You met him once when he traveled here before the Ashwea Awhidi."

Tar'sa looked away.

"I remember him," she said quietly.

"I do not wish to pry, nor do I wish to stir up painful memories. But you should know that Khon'Tor has confessed to what he did to you."

Tar'sa sighed. "I see."

"Come, sit next to me, please," and Urilla Wuti motioned her over and patted the sleeping map.

Tar'sa slowly took a seat next to the Healer.

"You never told anyone." Urilla Wuti said it as a statement.

"So, this is why you are here? To speak with me about that? No, I never told anyone. There did not seem to be a point. No one would have believed me. Why would a Leader as famous and powerful as Khon'Tor risk everything by committing such a crime? I know we do not mate outside of pairings, but if he had wanted to, I am sure there would have been some females who would have mated with him.

"It was a terrible few months, though, waiting to see if he had seeded me. Knowing if he had, that I would have years and years of worrying whether the offspring was his or my mate's. He was smart, that one. Afterward, he told me to mate with Knoton frequently, so that if I were seeded, Knoton would not suspect it might not be his. But then I still had the fear that if I had been seeded, the offspring might have had Khon'Tor's distinctive looks. What then?"

"So, your mate does not know. Nor suspect?"

"No. Over the past few years, I made peace with it as part of my journey. From then on, I mostly put it out of my mind. I have found a way to deal with it and have happiness in my life, regardless."

"We only recently learned of this, Tar'sa. If anyone had known sooner, we would have come to you then. It is a terrible burden to have to shoulder."

"Thank you for acknowledging that."

"I am also here to find out what punishment you wish delivered to Khon'Tor for what he did to you."

Tar'sa raised her eyebrows.

"Punishment? No punishment can make up for

what he did to me; no female should have to go through what I did, but I refused to let it ruin my life. You said he confessed?"

"Yes. Of his own accord, Khon'Tor confessed to the High Council."

"After this time, why would he do that? He had gotten away with it."

"He has been through some experiences that have changed him. I believe he is truly remorseful for what he did to you."

"I see. Well, I believe that people can change. And since there was no way of anyone finding out without his confessing, then I believe you that he does regret what he did to me."

Tar'sa stood up.

"Your reputation is impeccable, Healer. If you tell me he has changed, I believe you. What was done is done; I have moved on. Let the past stay buried where it belongs."

Tar'sa moved toward the doorway to leave, then turned back.

"One more thing. Please give him a message for me. Tell him that though I cannot understand why he committed such a crime against me, I have made peace with it. I moved on long ago. And please," she paused, "this is important. Tell him that I forgive him."

"You are a remarkable soul, Tar'sa. I will give him your message," said Urilla Wuti.

"So, since you came to speak with me, does this

mean you will be returning soon?"

"Yes. I will carry back to the High Council the message that you do not wish him punished. And I will deliver your message to Khon'Tor."

"Who else knows about this?"

"Only a handful of people. We have kept it as quiet as possible out of respect for the victims."

"Victims?" exclaimed Tar'sa. "He did this to more than me?"

"Yes. Does that change anything for you to know that?"

Tar'sa was silent a moment.

"No. Only that I hope the others have found their way through it, as I have. What he did was criminal. But if I had not learned to forgive him, it would have dominated my life. Perhaps even destroyed it, no doubt."

She paused a moment before continuing, "I will bring you something to eat after I have checked on High Protector Acaraho."

"Thank you. Ask him to come and see me as soon as he is able."

Acaraho came directly. "Have you already spoken with Tar'sa?"

"Yes. The opportunity came this morning. She does not want Khon'Tor punished. She somehow made peace with it long ago and has moved on.

And— She wants me to tell him that she forgives him."

Acaraho shook his head. "I did not expect that."

"Nor did I. This means we can return to the Far High Hills as soon as you wish."

"As soon as *you* are ready. You may still need a day's rest to recover."

"We can leave this morning. I am anxious to get back to Adia, and I know you are as well."

"I will let Lesharo'Mok know we are leaving soon, and I will check back with you shortly."

While Acaraho was gone, Urilla Wuti lay back on the sleeping mat and closed her eyes, reaching out to open a Connection with Adia. She shared an impression with her of Tar'sa's forgiveness of Khon'Tor and immediately felt the relief flow over Adia—for Tehya's sake.

The next day, Acaraho and Urilla Wuti returned. After checking in with Adia, Acaraho requested a meeting with Harak'Sar and Risik'Tar.

"I shared this information with Lesharo'Mok before I returned. Urilla Wuti met with Khon'Tor's victim at the Deep Valley. She does not want to inflict punishment on him; she says she made peace with it long ago. She also sent a personal message for Khon'-Tor, that she forgives him."

Both Leaders shook their heads.

"This is unexpected. It simplifies matters greatly, that is certain," said Harak'Sar. "Now we can proceed with the announcement that you are the new Leader of the High Rocks."

"I wish to refuse the appointment."

"You have made that clear. However, there is no one else more suited. Or even as well-suited. Commander, this is your mantle now. Accept it with honor and grace."

At that, Straf'Tor's words echoed in Acaraho's mind. *And you, my son. There are also challenges awaiting you. Find the strength to take your rightful place. Step out from the shadows of those who have gone before you.*

A chill ran up Acaraho's back. He heaved a huge sigh and nodded.

"Alright. I willingly accept the appointment of Leader of the High Rocks, and I will tell my mate as soon as possible. But it means there will be no Third Rank, as Adia is already Second Rank, but as the Leader's Mate, now Third Rank too. We will also need a new High Protector."

"We will work all that out later—one step at a time. I suggest we make plans to return to the High Rocks and make the announcement as soon as we have spoken with Khon'Tor and his mate about the news from the Deep Valley."

"Shall I bring Khon'Tor and Tehya here, or as he is still recovering, do you wish to go to them? I think Urilla Wuti should also be present."

"Go on ahead and tell them we are coming; it will give them time to prepare while knowing the report is coming."

Khon'Tor and Tehya braced themselves for the visit. Tehya sat close to her mate with both hands wrapped tightly around one of his.

Harak'Sar spoke first. "I will immediately put your minds at ease. The female from the Deep Valley does not wish for any punishment to be delivered. Furthermore, she sent a personal message to you, Khon'Tor."

It was Urilla Wuti's cue to step forward. "I had an opportunity to speak with her at length. She said that while she will never understand why you attacked her as you did, she has moved on. She has found a way to make peace with it and wishes the past to stay buried where it belongs. And she specifically wanted me to tell you that she forgives you."

Tehya clutched Khon'Tor's hand even tighter.

Khon'Tor raised his eyebrows. "I do not know what to say."

"She has made peace with what you did to her. She has moved on and does not want to dig up the past," Urilla Wuti reiterated.

"What happens now?" asked Tehya.

"As I have offered," said Harak'Sar, "you will be permitted to stay here at the Far High Hills. Your parents and family are here, Tehya. And this will be a safe place for Arismae to grow up. No one will know of your mate's crimes unless you speak of them. The rest of us are sworn to silence—for your sake and the sake of your offspring."

"For that, I am truly grateful," Khon'Tor said.

"As far as the leadership of the High Rocks goes, since there is no direct heir we can name, we are putting Acaraho in place as Leader."

Khon'Tor nodded. "You will make a fine Leader," he said.

"The people of the High Rocks need to hear this from you, though, Khon'Tor," said Harak'Sar. "So we ask that you and your family travel back to make the announcement. You will need to find a plausible reason for stepping down."

"His scars; they are healed but may never be completely haired over," Tehya pointed out.

"We will have one of the pattern-makers create some type of covering. It may raise questions, but the scars would raise more. Acaraho, you are nearly the same build as Khon'Tor. They can use you for sizing."

"Thank you for your consideration. It is more than I deserve," said Khon'Tor.

"Yes, it is," said Harak'Sar. "Make no mistake, Khon'Tor. Your crimes are despicable. But for your mate's sake and that of your offspring, I will do my best to put them from my mind. If one of your victims can find a way to forgive you, I will also try.

"But," he added, "There is still the matter of the Overseer. We are not convinced that we know the reason behind his sudden hatred of you." And then he looked directly at Tehya, "For your sake, for the sake of your parents, and the sake of your daughter, we must get to the bottom of it and find a resolution."

Before they left, Tehya spoke up, "We have not been leaving our quarters. How are Adia and the offspring?"

"They are both fine. It is a male, but we have not named him yet."

"You must be so happy. I am so glad for you."

"Thank you. We are just not quite ready to share him with anyone else yet. I am sure you understand."

"Of course. Give Adia my love and let me know when I can visit her. If not, hopefully, I will get to see her when we return to the High Rocks."

"I have stopped fighting the idea of stepping into the leadership of our community," said Acaraho to his mate. "I thought you would want to know."

"What changed your mind?" Adia asked.

"When the apparition of Straf'Tor appeared, he spoke to the Sarnonn, to the People in general, and then to Khon'Tor and me. He told me that I need to step out of the shadows of those who have gone before and take my rightful place. In my heart, I know it is this of which he was speaking."

"I am pleased you have peace about it."

"We must leave for the High Rocks. They wish to make the announcement."

Adia closed her eyes. "Please bring Urilla Wuti. It is time we get some answers."

CHAPTER 8

Urilla Wuti and Adia prepared themselves to contact E'ranale. Stretched out side by side, they closed their eyes and opened the Connection to the Corridor.

This time, they found themselves in a meadow filled with lavender. The scent was far sweeter than anything known on Etera. As before, the experience was deeper, broader, richer than the life they knew. From behind a beautiful flowering Magnolia tree, stepped E'ranale.

"I am pleased to see you both. I have been waiting."

"My offspring. Our offspring—"

"Everything is as it should be, Adia. I reminded you of this during our last visit. You should know by now to trust your path."

"But—"

"The last time we spoke, I explained about the

Mothoc and the role of the Guardians. The six Guardian pairs were created not only to cleanse the Aezaitera, the creative life force that is constantly moving in and out of your realm—but also to protect Kthama and Kht'shWea. That is part of the purpose of their creation. Out of the mated pairs, new Guardians will be born. However, as I explained the last time, they will not be as powerful as a Mothoc Guardian, so, to keep Etera alive, more of them will be necessary than in the past. And they must be trained in their roles. At present, they know they have a calling, but they do not know what it is.

"Adia, when you entered the void after Khon'Tor and Tehya, what did you experience?"

"Loneliness, hopelessness, a separation that seemed to deepen with each passing moment. Had I followed Khon'Tor into krell?"

"Your Leader was not in krell, but he was on his way there. And Tehya's love for Khon'Tor was taking her with him. In the lowest depths of krell, there is only separation; there is no shared experience of others. By its nature, it is isolation and hopelessness and loneliness beyond that which a soul can bear. Had he made the full transition, there would have been no connecting with him. You would not have been able to find him in the darkness because the separation would have been complete. So, though here there is sharing of this experience of the Corridor, as you call it—which other cultures have called paradise—in krell, there is no shared experience.

There is only isolation and separation, and the bleak, dark unending night."

"So krell is real."

"Unfortunately, yes. krell is the ultimate separation from belonging. It is the place of the lost."

Before going on, E'ranale gave them a moment to take in what she had explained.

"All things exist as a state of consciousness," she continued. "Just as this place of beauty is a state of consciousness, so is krell. I spoke to you of the division brought by the Waschini's belief in scarcity and competition. That belief leads to separateness, to isolation, to the feeling that one is alone and not united with the rest of creation. Fear. And fear incites more fear, bringing more despair and more pain and more separation. Because of the limitations of your realm, it is easy for the belief in scarcity and lack to take hold. There are hard limits to provision, after all. Waters ebb and flow. When the seasons change, the trees no longer produce fruit. If the destructive thought grows for long enough, to where the balance is thrown off, and it overpowers the positive force that the Aezaitera bring in, then Etera could decay to where she will no longer support life."

Adia looked at Urilla Wuti, who was intently concentrating on what E'ranale was saying. "The role of the new Guardians is the same as the old; to cleanse the Aezaitera, the creative life force that is constantly moving in and out of your realm. But they must be trained. Adia, do you know who pulled you out when you went to rescue Khon'Tor and Tehya?"

"I heard a name—if you can call it hearing. It was more a recognition in my soul. *Pan*. Are you saying Pan will teach the new Guardians what they need to know? That she can reach out from the Corridor? I do not know why that surprises me, since Straf'Tor saved us by appearing on the battlefield."

"Pan does not need to reach out from the Corridor, Adia."

Urilla Wuti looked at E'ranale with wide eyes.

"Yes. Pan still walks Etera. Pan is a Guardian. Guardians are almost immortal. My daughter—Pan —has been waiting, marking the centuries for this time to come, when she can fill her role as the last of the Mothoc Guardians. She will guide the new Guardians and teach them to use their abilities. Kthama and Kht'shWea must be protected at all costs. Not only for the preservation of the 'Tor line, from which all natural-born Guardians come, but the primary vortex under both Kthama and Kht'sh-Wea, now more fully awakened since the opening of Kthama Minor, must be protected at all cost."

Adia said nothing, but she noted almost personal urgency in E'ranale's statements.

"When you return to Kthama, you will become far more aware of the magnetic well that now swells and rolls under both Kthama and Kht'shWea. Some of your watchers, who were already more attuned to

Etera's magnetic currents, have noticed it. The Sarnonn are aware of it and the Guardians even more so. It has always been there, but mostly dormant compared to its full potential. There are other vortexes on Etera, and ultimately, they are all connected like a giant web and they ebb and flow into each other. But the vortex under Kthama is the strongest and the primary. As I said, great power resides there."

Adia did not understand everything E'ranele was telling them but was too overcome by the news that Pan still lived to think of asking.

"But what of the bodies preserved in the chamber at Kht'shWea? One of them appears to be a Guardian. If they are immortal—?"

"That is true. The one you speak of is Moc'Tor. My mate. My beloved. The Father-Of-Us-All, as the Sarnonn refer to him. But that story is for another time. For now, return to your realm. As for Pan, she will make contact when the time is right. Tell the Commander that he will be supported in his new role. Return to the High Rocks."

"But my son—my offspring—?"

"You have a right to ask questions. I will not answer them now, but the answers *will* be provided in time, Adia. I promise you that."

Adia felt all her stress finally reaching an apex.

"I do not understand why you will not help us. You have answers but will not share them freely. Why can you not tell us what we need to know instead of letting us stumble through it, lost in the dark?"

"I understand your frustration. But if I give you the answers, I cheat you of your journey. Whether you realize it or not, there is always help for you along the way, but you alone can walk your path. The experiences mold and shape you, Healer. The experiences of one step prepare you for the next step, which guides you through the experiences that lie ahead of those. Here, there is no change. Everything that was or will be already is. But you are living in the realm of change and effect; your decisions affect your path and your path affects you. Spiritual growth can only take place on your realm, Adia. Because here, there is no change."

"How can everything that has ever happened, or will happen, or whatever you said, all exist at once? If that is true, how can there be any order here? How does any separate moment exist?"

"On Etera, if you are in your quarters and you leave to go to the common eating area, your living quarters still exist. They are still there; you are simply not experiencing them. That is what it is here. Everything exists at once, but you do not notice unless you focus your attention on it, and then you can, so to speak, enter that aspect of reality." With that, E'ranale motioned, and instead of the solitary Magnolia tree, an entire grove appeared instantly.

"So that is how people from the past, our past, like Lifrin, can appear."

"There is no past, no future; there is only now. This is also true in your realm, though, because of change, you believe time is passing. Here there is no change, so no time passes. Everything always is. Your focus, your soul's deepest intention, and the next step on your journey create what slice of it you experience."

Silence.

"It is time for you to return. You may share our conversation with your mate. As for your offspring, Adia, the answer will be provided. One step at a time. He is healthy. He is exactly who he is supposed to be. Trust your guidance. Trust that you are loved and cared for."

Adia felt herself returning to her body. Within a few moments, her spirit was back in Etera with Urilla Wuti lying beside her.

Urilla Wuti looked over at Adia. "I am not even going to *try* to explain that last part to the High Council," and Adia laughed with her.

"I know you are joking, Urilla Wuti, but there is wisdom in what you are saying. Perhaps, someday, they will be in a state of mind to hear it, but now they could not accept it. I think that is part of what happened with the Overseer. It was too much, too fast. He is a male of action, not musings."

"This life is not an easy one. But, oh, what a

journey it is turning out to be," the older Healer added.

"Even though I did not get the answers I wanted, I am more at peace now. At least I know that my son, *whatever he is*, he is not a mistake."

"You need to name him, Adia. You and Acaraho need to name him. And what of Nootau? He has been asking to see his brother for some time."

Adia sighed. "You are right. I cannot keep him a secret any longer. I may as well start with Nootau. As his brother, it is only right that Nootau gets to meet him first."

Adia went to find Acaraho and found him and Nootau talking together in the common eating area.

"Nootau," she said, "you have yet to meet your little brother. But I want to prepare you because, even though he is healthy, your brother is not exactly like the rest of us."

"So we will need your help, son, just as you helped Oh'Dar, who was also different," added Acaraho.

"So, may I see him now?"

"Yes, let us go to the Healer's Quarters. Iella has been watching him for me while Urilla Wuti and I took care of something."

As they all entered, Iella glanced up from her work.

"I am glad to see you, Adia. Have you come to fetch your son?"

"We thought it time that his big brother meets him."

Adia scooped the tiny offspring up out of his nest.

Nootau smiled profusely, then looked at his mother. "May I hold him?"

"Of course. Here," and she gently handed the offspring to Nootau. She glanced up at Acaraho, then back at Nootau as he cradled his brother.

"I had a dream about him," said Nootau out of nowhere as he fussed with the offspring's coverings. Both his parents unconsciously caught their breath.

"I had a dream that you named him An'Kru."

A chill ran up Adia's spine.

"When? When did you have this dream, son?" asked Acaraho once he had found his voice.

"It was some time ago—when Kthama Minor was opened."

"What happened? Was there anything else in that dream?"

"Yes, Father. I was in a beautiful meadow. More beautiful than you can imagine. I cannot explain how real everything was. It was so peaceful. I wanted never to leave. The colors were so intense that it was almost as if I could feel them. Even the sound of the birds was sweeter. Then a very, very tall female came to me. She was the one who told me his name. She was not quite Sarnonn, though. She was much larger, and she was more heavily covered in fur that was sparkling white. And it shimmered, like the lights in the sky sometimes do. Her face also looked different. I should have been afraid of her, but I was not. She said her name was Pan, and that my role in the future of the People would be very important. And that I needed to help An'Kru and look out for him, as I did for Oh'Dar."

Both Adia and Acaraho were speechless.

"Have you had other dreams like this?"

"Not like this one. It was more real—if you can understand that."

Adia nodded. "And you did not think to mention this dream?" She worded it very carefully, so it did not sound like an admonishment.

"Oh. I wanted to, Mama. So many times. But Pan told me not to. Not until I held him; she showed me a vision where I was sitting right here, looking at him just as I am now. She wanted me to know that everything is unfolding as it should be. She said that."

"I am proud of you, son," said Acaraho. "It must have been difficult to keep that secret for this long."

"I remember a while ago, at that Ashwea Awhidi, when I was to be paired with Nimida, the Overseer told me to withdraw my pairing request. He told me that sometimes I would be asked to do things without understanding why."

"Thank you for telling us all of this. Do you want me to take—An'Kru—back now?" his mother asked.

"Yes, here. I am going to stay for a while with Iella. She and I have become friends." Nootau glanced over at the new young Healer, who smiled, embarrassed, and lowered her eyes.

Adia and Acaraho looked at each other, and he raised one eyebrow. Then Acaraho nodded. "We are returning to our quarters."

"Do you wish to leave the offspring with me? You could perhaps use some time alone together," offered Iella. "If you wish, I will bring him back to you in a little while."

"Thank you, that is very considerate. Nootau, I believe we will be returning to the High Rocks soon."

A look of disappointment crossed Nootau's face. "Do I have to come?"

"There is going to be an important announcement, so yes, you do," said Acaraho. "But afterward, you can return to the Far High Hills whenever you wish; you are a grown male now. Just tell us you are going."

"So you know," added Adia, "as your mother, however old you are, I will always worry if I do not know your whereabouts."

"I had that figured out," he replied, and they all laughed.

Back in their quarters, Acaraho said, "I know I have not truly engaged with this whole E'ranale and the Corridor thing. But I have fully to concede the reality of it now. I do not mean that badly; you know I believe you. Only, now—"

"Now that you have heard it from another source, it is more real."

"Yes. But was Nootau talking about Pan, the last of the Mothoc Guardians—whom Bidzel mentioned? Was that who was in his dream?"

"Yes. Pan is the daughter of Moc'Tor and E'ranale. It was she who pulled me back from the depths of my connection with Khon'Tor and Tehya. I could not have returned on my own, and Urilla Wuti could not pull me out either. If it had not been for Pan, I would not have come back to you."

"Tell me the rest. I am now ready to listen with an open mind. I will not resist your calling any longer, just as I will no longer fight the leadership of the High Rocks."

They sat together for the rest of the afternoon and into the evening, and Adia told him everything —even how Pan was still alive somewhere on Etera and that she would be the one to teach the Sarnonn Guardians how to use their abilities.

When she had finished, and An'Kru was resting peacefully, they lay quietly together in each other's arms.

Akar'Tor could not stay at Kayerm. As cold-hearted as he was, even he found it lonely and filled only with bad memories. So he returned to the small cave where he had imprisoned Tehya. *I cannot survive on my own. Somehow I need to find others to join up with. But where? I know only of Kthama and Kayerm. I never heard them talk about any other communities, but surely they must exist. If so, would word about me have traveled to them? Is there anywhere I would be welcome?*

Akar'Tor made plans to gather enough supplies to set off on a journey into the vast unknown.

Time was drawing near for Acaraho, Adia, Nootau, Khon'Tor, and Tehya to return to the High Rocks. Harak'Sar, Risik'Tar, and Lesharo'Mok, who had since returned to the Far High Hills, sought out Acaraho to speak with him privately.

"We still have the matter of Kurak'Kahn's bitterness to resolve," said Harak'Sar. "Before you leave, we are going to meet with him to see if he will reveal any more than he has. Come with us."

"I must fetch something first," said Acaraho. "I will join you shortly."

Kurak'Kahn, still confined to his quarters, remained agitated. He stood up abruptly when the four entered.

"Khon'Tor and his mate are returning to the High Rocks," said Harak'Sar.

"Surely not as the Leader. I stripped Khon'Tor of that position."

"No, not as Adik'Tar. He will be telling the People of the High Rocks that he is stepping down and that Acaraho will be their new Leader. Khon'Tor has now paid for his crimes, and it is time for all of us to move on. Including you," said Risik'Tar.

"Maybe you are moving on, but I will not. You said Khon'Tor has paid for his crimes, but you are wrong. Not all of them."

There was dead silence, and Acaraho entered.

Kurak'Kahn returned to the sleeping mat and slumped over. His voice was low and shaky, "He did not even know her name. He did not know who she was or where she was from. A nameless maiden to be used as he wished and then discarded. Left to deal for the rest of her life with the emotional scars from what he did to her."

"What are you talking about?" asked Harak'Sar.

"Khon'Tor's third victim. Khon'Tor's third victim was my niece."

The Leaders locked eyes with each other.

"How do you know it was he? Did she tell you?" asked Risik'Tar.

Kurak'Kahn rested his head in his hands.

"She did not have to," he said. He dropped his hands and looked up at the others. "The circumstances spoke for themselves. Linoi asked to be paired soon after the Ashwea Awhidi. She and a longtime friend came forward. I performed the pairing myself. They had known each other all their lives and only fallen in love a year before. He wanted to be paired, but she resisted. Then, after the Ashwea Awhidi, she suddenly had a change of heart. Except that I understood too late; she feared Khon'Tor might have seeded her, and needed a pairing to explain the offspring."

He continued. "The time she was carrying the offspring was uneventful. It was only after he was born that Berak questioned its paternity. The offspring was darker-colored and heavily built. Nothing like either of them. Not even close to anyone on either side of their lines. I know both of their families, and that is a fact. Eventually, she broke down and told him what had happened. That she had been taken Without Her Consent."

Harak'Sar and Acaraho stood silent, waiting for him to continue.

"Berak did not believe her. He did not believe that any male would do such a thing. Instead, he believed she had lain with another and was covering up her sin with this lie. After all that time of knowing her, he did not know her at all. I knew Linoi well, and to think that she would make up such a lie or that she would have mated with another behind his back was unthinkable."

"Did he seek Bak'tah-Awhidi?"

"No. How I wish he had. Instead, Berak started

punishing Linoi. Neither her parents nor Larara and I had any idea it was happening. He became verbally cruel. Sadistic. Each time they argued, he threatened to kill the offspring. He tried to force her to tell him who she had mated with. She stuck to her story—that she had no idea; the male had worn a hood. She only knew that he was tall and muscular, but at the Ashwea Awhidi there were many males with that build. Berak became enraged, and finally, one day, he struck Linoi. When we found her, she was still unconscious, dried blood covering her face where he had hit her. When Linoi came around, she told us what had been going on between them. We immediately started looking for him. But by then, he was long gone, with their offspring."

Afraid to hear the answer, Harak'Sar had to ask anyway, "Where are they all now?"

"As far as Berak and the offspring are concerned, we do not know. We searched everywhere, but he had quite a head start before we found Linoi. And we are a small community; we have never had enough extra males to place the watchers that you do. And even if we had, as the father, there was no real alarm in his leaving and taking the offspring with him.

"As for Linoi, she blamed herself, convinced that Berak had taken her offspring to murder him. She could not live with it. She felt utterly alone and powerless, inconsolable. Last month we found her body at the bottom of a ravine."

There was a shocked silence.

"With all respect, Kurak'Kahn, that does not mean she took her own life. It could have been Berak. Or an accident," interjected Risik'Tar.

"*Still trying to protect Khon'Tor*? No, she could not live with what Khon'Tor did to her; everything that unfolded was because of his monstrous act. How many lives has Khon'Tor ruined? And we do not know if he is being honest about the number. Perhaps there are more."

"Urilla Wuti was right, Kurak'Kahn, you should have recused yourself," said Harak'Sar. "You took an oath of objectivity—we all did. We all sometimes wrestle with the situations presented to us, but you seem to have no struggle at all about this one. Your judgment is impaired; you are too close to the situation. That is why you wanted to continue with the lashings. You wanted to see him die."

"It is what he deserves."

"You agreed that the females would determine the punishment. You accepted that," said Harak'Sar.

"Well, we will never hear from his third victim, now will we? And since she is dead because of him, he deserves to die as well," said Kurak'Kahn bitterly.

"The loss of your niece is a terrible blow," said Harak'Sar. "There is no doubt. Yet you have no proof that she died at her own hand. She managed to live with what was done to her; you do not know if she did take her own life—that it was Berak's abuse that drove her to it. You do not know where the offspring is. There is a chance that he might still be alive somewhere. As nasty as Berak may be, to harm an offspring is a darker act than I can imagine any of us capable of," added Harak'Sar.

"You are right, Harak'Sar." Lesharo'Mok turned back to Kurak'Kahn, "Yours is a small community. I would be willing to send searchers out to see if there is any trail of the offspring. At least it would give you and your mate some small relief."

"So would I," said Risik'Tar.

Harak'Sar nodded his agreement.

"And this is in return for my silence?" scoffed Kurak'Kahn.

"Because it is the right thing to do," the Leader of the Far High Hills replied.

Kurak'Kahn let out a huge sigh. "It has helped to share everything with you, and if you will do that, then, for Larara's sake, I will keep my silence. I am not utterly unreasonable; part of me accepts what you are saying, but the anger in my heart is almost impossible to manage."

"Then an agreement has been struck," said Lesharo'Mok.

"Not quite yet," said Acaraho, who stepped forward and brought out something from behind his back.

"Do you recognize this?" he held it up to the others.

"That looks like the whip the Overseer used on Khon'Tor," said Harak'Sar.

"How long have you had this, Kurak'Kahn? How

long have you been carrying it around with you?" Acaraho demanded.

Kurak'Kahn looked away.

"There is more to the story than Kurak'Kahn is telling us," Acaraho said, looking at the other Leaders. "This is no ordinary whip. Through wet forming, it has been altered to imbed obsidian shards in the stripes. It is an old practice, and this is what caused so much damage so quickly."

"That whip was banned generations ago for being too brutal," said Harak'Sar. "Where did you get it?"

"You had it made specifically for this purpose, did you not?" demanded Acaraho.

Kurak'Kahn glared at the High Protector but said nothing.

"Let me explain for the others then, since you seem reluctant to speak," said Acaraho. "You had this made and brought it with you intending all along to use it on Khon'Tor. Abusing your authority as Overseer, you were going to accuse him of your niece's death, find him guilty, and decide the punishment yourself. You were hoping you could convince us that he did it, counting that our outrage at learning this would make us override due process. Only he made it easy for you when he came forward and confessed on his own. I thought you wanted him whipped outside to avoid the splattering of blood everywhere. But the real reason was so that the shards would be scattered after several blows and not be discovered.

The only problem—you overlooked the probability that some of them would become embedded in Khon'Tor's flesh, which is where the Healers found them when they cleaned his wounds."

"How long have you known this, Acaraho?" asked Lesharo'Mok.

"Adia told me just before she gave birth. If Khon'Tor had died, as Kurak'Kahn had intended, it would not have been discovered as there would have been no need to clean the wounds. When Adia told me, I went back and found the weapon, which Kurak'Kahn no doubt intended quietly to take back with him. And none of us would have known the better."

"This is an abomination. You planned this all along, and not based on facts, but on your presumptions of Khon'Tor's guilt. Your abuse of your authority is worse than we thought," said Risik'Tar.

"What Khon'Tor did was an abomination, but what you have done is no less a crime," added Harak'Sar.

Kurak'Kahn still refused to speak.

"So *here* is the agreement," declared Acaraho. "You will hold your silence about Khon'Tor's crimes as well as your unsubstantiated accusations toward him about your niece. If you do not, then I will bring you up on charges for the attempted murder of Khon'Tor. The other Leaders here will bear witness to the events, as will the Healers, as will this weapon. You will be publicly disgraced, and your legacy will be one of dishonor and shame. Your mate will be brokenhearted, realizing the cruelty of which you are capable. As for the missing offspring, I agree that we should all help try to find him. Those are the conditions. I suggest you accept them."

Kurak'Kahn said quietly. "I accept the conditions."

"An agreement has now been struck," said the new Leader of the High Rocks. "I strongly suggest you hold yourself to it, Kurak'Kahn."

Then Acaraho turned and left the room, followed by the three other Leaders.

The time to return home to Kthama had finally come. Khon'Tor had been outfitted with what turned out to be a quite handsome piece of apparel, fashioned from hide and secured with straps that crossed his chest. Though he had told no one of it, it reminded him of the piece Oh'Dar had made for him to support the weapon he still intended to put to use —someday. Acaraho had also asked for something similar to what Nootau had started wearing, not only in support of Nootau but also to soften the shock of Khon'Tor's wrappings. Tehya had talked him into adding a loincloth as she said otherwise it looked off-balance.

Tehya, Arismae, and Khon'Tor traveled alone ahead of Acaraho and the others. Though the Deep

Valley was only a day's travel, they stopped there and stayed overnight.

Nootau said his goodbyes to Iella, and the tenderness between them was not missed by either his parents or Urilla Wuti. Yet again, Adia was deeply grateful that the High Council had lifted the restriction for Healers to pair.

Acaraho, Adia, Nootau, and Urilla Wuti also overnighted at the Deep Valley.

Once they had left the Deep Valley, they re-entered the tunnel along the Mother Stream for the rest of the trip.

Finally, they all reached home. Adia nursed An'Kru and made him comfortable, and then they curled up together, enjoying the comfort and bliss of being home once more.

The next morning, Acaraho let word be spread that there would be a general assembly that afternoon. Then, on Khon'Tor's request, he and Harak'Sar went to speak with Haan.

Haan was sharing the morning meal in the common eating area at Kht'shWea. Haaka and Kalli were at his table. Ordinarily, the Leader would have risen to greet visitors but did not wish to tower over them.

He gestured toward the seating, but both

Harak'Sar and the High Protector remained standing.

After Haan had asked after Adia, Acaraho spoke. "We have all returned to Kthama. There will be an important announcement this afternoon, and Khon'Tor would like for you to attend. You may bring whichever of your leadership you wish. The High Council members have returned to Kthama specifically for this purpose."

"Send a messenger when it is time, and we will attend."

Acaraho's eyes swept the room. "This will be a historic event; I must invite Bidzel and Yuma'qia."

"They are still busy at the Wall of Records. They have a bottomless appetite for history and discovery."

"With your permission, I will speak with them now."

Haan gestured down the hallway, "You know the way, Commander."

Acaraho and Harak'Sar continued down the cool tunnel until they found the two researchers in the Wall of Records, just as Haan had said. Bidzel was climbing off the high scaffolding, and Yuma'qia called up to him, "We have visitors."

Bidzel dusted off his hands as the two walked over to Acaraho and Harak'Sar. "Is Khon'Tor with you?" he asked.

"He has returned with us to Kthama, yes."

"We continue to make discoveries and are anxious to share them."

"You mentioned this when you revealed that for some time, the leadership was passed through the females," said Acaraho. He walked absentmindedly over to the wall and looked it up and down. "I am impressed that you can figure this out at all."

As he was glancing away, something caught his eye.

"That mark there. What is that?" He pointed to the one in question.

"That is a family mark, just as many of the others are. Does it mean something to you?"

"Yes. I have seen that all my life. It is my family mark; I know this for a fact. It is one of the few things I know about my past."

Bidzel and Yuma'qia looked at each other.

"Are you sure, Commander?"

"It is the same mark as is on my Keeping Stone. Is it significant?"

"If that is your family mark, High Protector, then you are directly descended from the line of Straf'Tor."

Harak'Sar marched briskly over to the wall, practically pushing Bidzel out of the way, "*Where*? Show me what mark you are referring to."

Bidzel climbed a short way back up the scaffolding and pointed directly at the etching.

Harak'Sar followed him up and stood studying it

in detail. "Do you have your Keeping Stone in your quarters?" he asked Acaraho.

"Yes. Do you wish me to fetch it?"

"No. It will be faster if we all go there—if you do not mind the intrusion into your personal space?"

"By all means."

Harak'Sar turned to Bidzel and Yuma'qia, "Please, come with us."

It took a short while for them to return to Kthama, during which no one spoke.

When they reached his quarters, Acaraho turned to the others. "If you do not mind, let me bring the stone out to you. My mate is not prepared for company."

Acaraho returned with his Keeping Stone, which he handed carefully to Bidzel. Bidzel looked at it closely and passed it to Yuma'qia, who also inspected the stone before handing it to Harak'Sar.

"It is the same mark," Bidzel announced.

Yuma'qia nodded agreement.

"What do you know of your family history, Commander?" asked Harak'Sar, handing the stone back to Acaraho.

"Very little. I was raised by the family of First Guard Awan."

"We all agree it is the same mark; there is no mistaking it. You are a descendent of the House of 'Tor."

"I am of the 'Tor bloodline?"

Harak'Sar shook his head and snorted. "I do not know what to say. Truly."

Acaraho thought again of Straf'Tor's remarks. *"And you, my son. There are also challenges awaiting you. Find the strength to take your rightful place. Step out from the shadows of those who have gone before you."*

"This must be part of our announcement this afternoon. Bidzel and Yuma'qia, you would have been asked to attend regardless, but now your attendance is required. When the messenger comes for Haan and those who will be attending with him, I will let them know to collect you also."

"If you will excuse me, I must speak with my mate," said Acaraho.

The other males left, and he re-entered his quarters.

"I heard you speaking outside. It is true then, you are of the House of 'Tor?" asked Adia.

"Apparently. So much was lost when the Mothoc sealed Kthama Minor. The break in the records, in our knowledge—"

"This should put your mind at ease. You are entitled by blood to the leadership of the High Rocks."

"Now I understand Straf'Tor's message," said Acaraho. "Are you pleased that I have accepted the leadership?" he asked.

"I am pleased that you have made peace with it, my love," Adia answered.

Acaraho glanced around the room, "How is little An'Kru?"

"He is peacefully playing with his toes. Since he is awake, I think it is time for him to meet Nadiwani; would you mind bringing her here?"

Within a little while, Acaraho had returned with the Helper.

Nadiwani rushed to Adia and hugged her. "When did you get back home? I have missed you so much; thank goodness you have returned. And you have had your offspring. May I hold him? Nootau seems thrilled to have a little brother to look after."

Acaraho interrupted, "I am going with Harak'Sar and the researchers to speak with Lesharo'Mok and Khon'Tor. I will find you later, Saraste'."

Adia smiled at her mate and returned her attention to Nadiwani.

"Perhaps you can help me find a way to introduce him to the rest of Kthama."

Nadiwani walked over to the offspring and folded the wrapping away from him. She stared for a long time. Then she pulled him up out of his coverings and looked him over—his tiny fingers and toes, his eyes and hair—and then re-wrapped him warmly and cradled him in her arms.

"Remember, they accepted Oh'Dar. They will accept this one too. I suggest that you get it over with, Adia, instead of tiptoeing around it. There is a meeting this afternoon, and I believe you should introduce him then."

"Oh. I am not sure."

"I am. The longer you worry about this, the bigger it will become. I have no explanation, and I do not believe you do, or you would have told me. He is truly an enigma."

"I have a theory, but I am not ready to talk about it," Adia answered.

"What does Urilla Wuti think about when and how to introduce him?"

"She would agree with you about getting it over with. I will consider it; there is still some time before the announcement."

"Can you tell me what it is about?"

"Khon'Tor is stepping down from the leadership. The High Council is appointing Acaraho to be Leader in his stead."

Nadiwani grew silent for a moment

"Acaraho will make a great Leader," she finally said. "We knew they would have to make an exception to the Leader's bloodline unless there was some way for Nootau to be acknowledged."

"I should be used to the surprises by now," said Adia, "but I am not. The two researchers just revealed that Acaraho is a descendent of Straf'Tor. So he is 'Tor after all."

"Acaraho is of the House of 'Tor? Do you realize that this opens the door for Nootau? Since everyone believes that Acaraho is his father—Nootau is also 'Tor.'"

"But Acaraho is not his father," Adia frowned. "Khon'Tor is."

"A minor detail. The bloodline is intact; that is what is of importance. And I politely disagree with you. In every way that matters, Acaraho is Nootau's father."

Adia grew silent. "The truth should not be a burden. If I live five hundred years, I will never figure out how to make peace with less than complete honesty. Nimida and Nootau still do not know they are brother and sister."

"We are imperfect beings; we make mistakes. And because we make mistakes, the truth can be hurtful, even damaging. In a perfect world, the truth would be enough. But this life is a struggle, and the answers do not always fall into place. Perhaps our willingness to grapple with such dilemmas is enough to redeem us from our imperfection. Perhaps in time, you will yet find a way to tell them."

Both the Healer and her Helper—her dear friend —shared a moment of silent communion. Finally, Adia said, "I believe Nootau favors Urilla Wuti's niece, Iella. She has been apprenticing on and off with Urilla Wuti for some time and has recently taken her place as Healer."

"That is good to hear. You have not been at Kthama to see it," said Nadiwani, "but Nimida and

Tar have grown close. I would not be surprised if they ask to be paired."

A smile crossed Adia's lips.

Then Nadiwani asked, "How are Khon'Tor and Tehya and Arismae?"

"I believe they will be content to reside at the Far High Hills where Tehya's family is."

Carefully moving a stray wisp of hair from his face, Nadiwani rocked An'Kru as they continued speaking.

"He seems very good-natured. I will let you rest now, but I will stand with you at the assembly and support whatever you decide—to introduce him there or not."

"Thank you, dear friend."

Everyone was assembled in the Great Chamber. The air bristled with expectation. It was an unprecedented occasion; even all the watchers had been briefly pulled inside for the announcement. Tehya was sitting near the front with Adia, Nadiwani, Mapiya, Nootau, Nimida, and Tar. Acaraho was standing on the podium with Harak'Sar, Lesharo'Mok, and the two researchers. Haan, with Haaka and his chosen followers—ten of them in all—stood off to the side. Everyone eyed the covering Acaraho sported, so similar to Nootau's.

All heads turned as Khon'Tor entered from the

back, his Leader's Staff in his hand. He walked as before, with power and presence. The crowd immediately took in his new, comparatively ornate wraps. The females exchanged looks—raised eyebrows and shared nods and smiles.

Khon'Tor took the stage and turned to face the crowd. He raised his left hand to speak, and the crowd fell immediately silent. "We have returned to Kthama."

A cheer welled up from the crowd, and it was all Khon'Tor could do to maintain his composure. He nodded, "Thank you. Thank you for your welcoming support. It means more than you can realize. Much has happened since we evacuated Kthama. In time, the story of the confrontation with the Sarnonn will become legend. I hope you will carry it forward through our future generations; let them understand that it is not a fable, nor a story to entertain the offspring. Let them know that it truly happened— just as it has happened that the Sarnonn have returned to become our brothers and protectors."

Khon'Tor paused a moment.

"Oh'Dar of the People has already begun teaching some of you and your offspring how to make and interpret the marks of the Waschini, so we will no longer be dependent on flawed memory for the records of our history. The past few years have seen monumental changes, and they must be preserved in a less fallible manner than stories passed on from generation to generation. While we have simple markings that we can use to convey ideas, and the markings used to show family lines, we have nothing intricate enough to make records of any complexity. History must be faithfully recorded for the benefit of future generations. Willingly embrace this change, I ask you."

Khon'Tor took a few steps to the side. He looked down for a moment and then back up. He continued.

"You have been through much and should be commended for your faithfulness to each other and to us, your Leaders. Hopefully, an age of peace is opening up for our people as we join together in brotherhood with Haan's people."

"Change is the nature of life. Many times, change is for the best, though that does not mean it is easy. So, with difficulty and full awareness of the fact that this will no doubt come as a shock to you, I am announcing that I am stepping down from my position as Leader of the High Rocks."

The room fell into complete silence as everyone looked at each other. Then a murmur rolled through the crowd.

"No, why?" someone shouted.

"Please, Khon'Tor, do not abandon us!" someone else called out. Remarks of dismay arose for several moments.

Khon'Tor slowly raised his hand for silence, knowing that the next few heartbeats would be his last as Leader of the High Rocks.

"Thank you. I appreciate the sentiment, as does

my mate, Tehya. I know it is unprecedented, but we are living in unprecedented times. The time has come for Tehya and me to focus on our life together. And so, also has come the time for new leadership. We will be moving to the Far High Hills, where Tehya's parents and family live. Harak'Sar has extended his hospitality to us, and we have accepted. We will remain here a few days to transition leadership of the High Rocks, but then we will be leaving. I will remember you all warmly; It has been my greatest honor to serve as your Adik'Tar. I hope you will forgive me for my failings, and I know they were many. I hope you will support the next Leader of the High Rocks as unfailingly as you have supported me."

Khon'Tor stood a moment and let his gaze travel across the crowd. Many faces were drawn, some frowning; more than a few of the females were trying not to cry. Others were openly crying. Many of the males' faces were somber. His eyes fleetingly caught Kayah and Akule at the back, and he wished he could undo what he had done to her. *Perhaps my leaving will help her now find peace.*

He silently thanked Harak'Sar for allowing him to withdraw with honor. He did not deserve it but was deeply grateful—especially for the sakes of Tehya and Arismae.

After one last sweeping look, he said, "Harak'Sar?"

Once again, people started talking amongst

themselves.

Harak'Sar stepped forward and waited for them to settle a bit before he spoke. "As Khon'Tor has said, this change in leadership is truly unprecedented. As you know, leadership has always been passed on through the bloodline. And with Khon'Tor having no ready heir, we were left with a situation where, regardless of bloodline, we had to appoint someone to be Leader of the High Rocks. Inside the Sarnonn cave system, Kht'shWea, there is a large chamber with a wall on which have been captured records from the distant past. These records show the descendants of the Ancients, Moc'Tor and Straf'Tor, the Mothoc ancestors who once lived at Kthama. Our two researchers who have been studying the wall have uncovered an unexpected lineage in the 'Tor line. We were shocked this morning to learn that the new Leader we selected is of the 'Tor blood. The two researchers, Bidzel and Yuma'qia, who stand with me now, will affirm that the next Leader of Kthama is of 'Tor descent."

Bidzel and Yuma'qia stepped forward. Yuma'qia looked as if he might pass out.

Bidzel cleared his throat. "It is true. The chosen new Leader is of 'Tor descent."

Glances were exchanged, but the crowd remained silent. Eyes traversed the room, trying to determine who the next Leader was.

"So let us continue with the transfer of authority. High Protector Acaraho, please step forward."

Acaraho stepped over to stand between Khon'Tor and Harak'Sar.

"Let the record show that Khon'Tor relinquishes his leadership of the High Rocks, and passes it to Acaraho'Tor, former High Protector of the High Rocks."

At that moment, for the last time, Khon'Tor slammed his Leader's Staff into the ground. The crack echoed through the Great Chamber.

Then he slowly turned to Acaraho and handed him the Leader's Staff, the staff of the House of 'Tor. Acaraho wrapped his hand around the staff as Khon'Tor released it.

The mantle had been passed.

Lesharo'Mok turned and loudly announced, "Kah-Sol 'Rin. *It is done.*"

Khon'Tor let his eyes sweep the crowd, taking one last look at the People he had led for most of his life. Then he looked down at Tehya, took her hand, and stepped forward.

The People of the High Rocks solemnly watched as Khon'Tor exited the stage and moved to the back of the room. They remained respectfully silent, struggling with a rising tide of mixed emotions.

Adia turned her head away as Khon'Tor walked past. Despite everything, despite her happiness for her mate, tears stung her eyes. She would not allow herself to look at Tehya, either. It was the end of Khon'Tor's legendary leadership, that which she had fought so hard through the decades to protect. She was grateful it had not ended in public shame, but it was the end of an age.

Acaraho extended his hand to Adia, and she carried An'Kru with her to the front.

Then he spoke his first words as Leader of the High Rocks. "Nothing I could say can do justice to this moment. I know you are filled with emotion, as am I. As is Adia. Except in the apprenticeship of an heir, it has never happened that leadership has passed from one to another during a standing Leader's lifetime. I need you to know that I never sought the leadership of the High Rocks. I have been content to serve in my capacity as High Protector and have been honored to do so. In fact, when I was told the High Council intended to appoint me to be Leader, I refused. Or, *I tried to refuse* would be correct to say, as an order from the High Council is outside my authority to deny. Their appointment was reaffirmed by the revelation from the researchers that I share the same bloodline as Khon'Tor. So, I stand here, with my mate and our new offspring, ready to serve you in my new capacity. And I know that along with us, you all wish Khon'Tor and Tehya happiness in their new life at Far High Hills. Their absence from Kthama will leave an open place in each of our hearts and we will never forget their leadership and years of service."

Adia looked around the room, and her eyes fell on Nadiwani and Urilla Wuti; she could feel them reassuring her that it was time for her to introduce An'Kru to the community. She swallowed hard, said a prayer to the Great Mother, and looked at her mate for confirmation. Acaraho nodded, and Adia took a step forward.

"Many of you remember the day, years ago, that Oh'Dar was revealed to everyone. The shock of having a Waschini offspring in our midst was nearly as powerful as the fact that I, your Healer, had broken Second Law by bringing him here. But you all found it in your hearts to forgive me and to accept him, and for that, I will always be grateful. And now, I stand here before you today, ready to introduce you to our new offspring. I do not have answers to the questions you will want to ask. I can only pray that you will extend to him the same love and acceptance that you extended to Oh'Dar. We are living in wondrous times, times which have brought us many challenges as well as many joys."

Adia turned so that her new offspring was facing the audience and pulled back the covering from his face.

The crowd gasped, nearly in one voice, then fell silent. Adia's heart stopped, and she squeezed her eyes tightly shut to cut off the tears. She had already been through the heartbreak and challenge of raising one different offspring. She knew something of the difficult path ahead of An'Kru, and her heart wept for him.

She looked down at her son and smoothed back his silver-white hair. He curled his tiny fingers around one of hers, his pale, almost translucent skin standing out in stark contrast to her darker tones. Overwhelming love filled her heart, and she knew she would protect her silver-colored offspring with her life if need be.

As if stunned, lost for what to say or do, no one moved. Then everyone's attention was drawn to motion over to the side as, simultaneously, Haan and all the followers he had brought with him dropped to one knee and bowed their heads. Their huge bodies then become still, lowered in what looked like homage. Everyone looked around, hoping for an answer to what was happening.

Haan then slowly looked up and returned to his feet. Raising one hand over his head, he loudly declared, "An'Kru."

Adia looked at Acaraho. "Did you tell Haan our son's name?" she whispered.

"I did not. I have told no one," Acaraho whispered back.

Haan turned solemnly to his group and motioned them to rise. Then, reverently and slowly, he moved toward Adia. Once he started moving, everyone's eyes were trained on him as he crossed the hard rock floor to stand by the Healer.

"Haan, I do not understand. How did you know

his name?"

"He is An'Kru," Haan said, staring at the offspring. "He is *The One Promised*. He is the Seventh of the Six, the one who will open the path to Wrak-Ashwea."

Haan turned back to his people and declared, "The prophecy has been fulfilled. An'Kru'Tor has come. An'Kru'Tor has come to lead us into the Age of Light."

Adia and Acaraho looked at each other, and then Adia found Urilla Wuti and saw her smiling and shaking her head in shared amazement. E'ranale's obscure phrase came back to Adia. *"The Order of Functions."*

Everything is changing. Great Mother, give me the strength to bear the mantle you have placed upon me and upon Acaraho. And help us to guide An'Kru on the path that lies before him, whatever that may be. Help me to continually remind myself of your guidance and grace as we face whatever lies ahead for us and our People.

At the back of the chamber, with his beloved mate at his side, Khon'Tor watched Acaraho and Adia at the front of the room, Acaraho standing in the place where Khon'Tor had stood for years. Now Adik'Tar and First Choice of the High Rocks, their chapter was just opening at the same time as his and Tehya's was now closing.

AN INTERVIEW WITH THE CHARACTERS

I first spoke with Khon'Tor.

LR: Now that Series One is drawing to a close, how do you feel?

KT: How should I feel? I have lost my leadership at the High Rocks. Yes, I would give it all up for Tehya, as I said, but I am still struggling with no longer being a Leader. And it has not ended—it is only a pause. You are writing Series Two, correct? How long is *that* going to take?

LR: Yes, I have already started Series Two.

KT: I am not even in Series Two.

LR: No, but I have decided there will be a Book Ten, and you are in it. Do not be curt with me, Khon'-Tor. I gave you life.

KT: I did not realize all you Waschini were so touchy.

LR: I know enough to realize that calling me Waschini is not a compliment.

KT: You had me whipped. I almost died, and so did Tehya. I am still adjusting to everything. And these wraps you have put me into are not comfortable.

LR: You will get used to them.

KT: They are not going away?"

LR: No. Since you just called me a Waschini, they are most certainly not.

(Unfortunately, Khon'Tor got up and stormed off, ending the interview.)

"See you in Book Ten!" I called out after him.

Acaraho was next. He took a seat.

A: I did not see this coming.

LR: What part?

A: All of it. I never knew much about my past. I still do not. I thought I was able to let that go, but I am not sure now.

LR: You have a son of your own bloodline!

A: Yes, but you had to make him weird, though.

LR: Oh, I say you are doing all right. You have Adia, you are now Leader of the High Rocks, and you have a bloodline son. Nootau can now be trained as heir to the High Rocks if you wish, since your being 'Tor paves the way for him. Oh'Dar is paired, and soon he and Acise will have offspring. And in my defense, I do not think 'weird' is a fair term. That is not like you, Acaraho.

A: You are right; I am not usually negative. But it has been a rough road since Book Five when Haan showed up with Akar'Tor and Hakani. I was hoping for a little peace, but now, being the Leader and with An'Kru as he is, that looks doubtful. I will be rested in time for the next book, I promise. When will that be?

LR: I am working on it. Enjoy the break and build up your strength. There is a lot more to come. We still have Series Three coming after Series Two.

A: I heard you talking with Khon'Tor. Are the males going to have to start wearing wraps now?

LR: It looks likely. Do you have a preference, though?

A: I would be fine either way. I suppose Khon'Tor looked smart in them. Nootau took the lead already, and I wore one to support Khon'Tor. I think they could catch on. I have one request, though.

LR: What is that?

A: Please, none of those Waschini foot coverings. Oh'Dar continually complains about how much they hurt when he has to wear them.

LR: A terrible invention, I agree. Alright, that is a deal; you will never have to wear those. Please send in Adia next—and go get some rest.

The final interview was with Adia.

LR: Adia, how are you feeling now that you know An'Kru is who he is supposed to be, and everything is falling into place?

ADIA: Much relieved, thank you. The conversations with E'ranale have helped a lot. And, throughout, having Urilla Wuti with me. I am still worried about Nimida and Nootau, though.

LR: I know. Life is not perfect—not even in fiction. I wish I had an answer for you.

ADIA: You do not? If you do not, who does?

LR: I will think of something, I promise. So far, I have not messed anything up too badly, have I?

ADIA: No, it appears all to be working out. So there will be a break for us now until the next Series?

LR: Not quite. As I said to Khon'Tor, I have decided there will be a Book Ten.

ADIA: Oh, great! Leigh?

LR: Yes, Adia?

ADIA: Thank you for bringing me to life.

LR: You are welcome. Rest assured, Adia; you have many adventures to come. And even after these series are over, you will live forever in the hearts of the many readers who have grown to love you. I can promise you that.

ADIA: Thank you, Leigh.

PLEASE READ

Dear Readers,

When I started this series, I didn't know how far it would go. And now here we are up to Book Nine. After Book Seven, I envisioned the series would end here, but as you can see this is not a really great stopping off point. I fear hate mail. Just kidding. Okay maybe not kidding.

As a result, my new plan for closing this series is that it will end with Book Ten: Endings and Beginnings. We'll see how well that goes.

If you would like to be notified about Book Ten and any other offerings, there are several ways you can stay in touch:

Email me at leigh@leighrobertsauthor.com

Join the mailing list by signing up at: https://www.subscribepage.com/theeterachroniclessubscribe

Join me on Facebook at The Etera Chronicles

Visit my author website at LeighRobertsauthor.com

Thank you for staying this journey with me! As long as people keep reading and leaving positive reviews, I have a lot more stories inside me waiting to be written.

Blessings—Leigh

ACKNOWLEDGMENTS

I lost my oldest brother, Bob, the month before this book was published. Bobby was nearly grown by the time I came along. I do not have a lot of memories of him from when I was growing up because he married and moved out of the house while I was still very young. But what I do remember is precious.

Bobby was the kind of person who would have you laughing halfway through a story and not even know why. He didn't even have to get to the punch-line or point of it – he was just naturally funny. He had a mechanical mind and enjoyed taking things apart and putting them back together. He loved electronics. My Aunt Elsie would not go into his bedroom because she feared for her life—afraid she would get electrocuted by all the gizmos he had disassembled that were scattered about.

He would entertain me and our brother Richard with stories of Sam Stove, Perky Percolator, Frochie Bugs, and Tallimosis Worms. He would take us out among the many trees where we lived and tell us stories about the Great White Apes who lived high in the treetops. Sometime during the telling of the tale, he would reach around the back of the tree and knock on the trunk with a stick. "Listen! Did you hear that?!" We never caught him doing it. Our eyes would get wide with astonishment that, even though we could not see them, they were 'up there' somewhere.

Above all, he was a devoted man of faith and a wonderful father to his three girls. I often wondered what I could have become had I had the guidance and attention that he gave them. They know they were blessed, but with no comparison, they will never fully realize how much. But perhaps that is a blessing itself, as they never knew the suffering that others of us experienced, those of us who were not so lucky to have a supportive, attentive, loving, and affectionate father such as he was.

Bobby never read any of my books. But he knew I had become an author, and he knew he was a huge influence on me during the short time we shared the same roof.

A heartfelt thank you to my readers, who, when I

posted that I had lost him, reminded me that Bobby waits for me in the Corridor.